The Kinley Legacy

From business to forever!

The Kinley company has been *the* prestige brand in British fashion for more than a century, but a series of bad investments has left the coffers nearly bare and the company in need of a miracle.

Now, to right the wrongs of their parents and save the Kinley name and legacy, the estranged Kinley siblings—Jonathan, Olivia and Caleb—will have to set aside their differences to come together and show the world what "family" really means.

Escape to the Cotswolds in Jonathan's story:

Reunion with the Brooding Millionaire

Available now!

And prepare to embark on an adventure in London and a holiday in Lake Como in

Olivia's and Caleb's stories

Coming soon from Harlequin Romance!

Dear Reader,

Welcome to The Kinley Legacy! I hope you enjoy getting to know this family as much as I have.

They were inspired by my own sprawling, messy bunch of siblings and our habit of camping out in any house big enough to accommodate us as often as we can. We don't encounter quite as much drama and heartache as the Kinleys, and our parents have yet to slip away to South America (because they know we would follow them and demand a spare room), but being a part of a big family is such a huge part of who I am that I couldn't resist exploring it here.

As I was writing this story, we decamped to the Cotswolds in real life—a trip delayed by COVID for a year—and this story is suffused with the magic of that beautiful part of the world, and the love, squabbles and silliness of being stuck with your grown-up siblings for a week.

Lots of love,

Ellie

X

Reunion with the Brooding Millionaire

Ellie Darkins

—

HARLEQUIN®
Romance™

Recycling programs
for this product may
not exist in your area.

ISBN-13: 978-1-335-40704-7

Reunion with the Brooding Millionaire

Copyright © 2022 by Ellie Darkins

This edition published by arrangement with Harlequin Books S.A.

For questions and comments about the quality of this book,
please contact us at CustomerService@Harlequin.com.

Harlequin Enterprises ULC
22 Adelaide St. West, 41st Floor
Toronto, Ontario M5H 4E3, Canada
www.Harlequin.com

Printed in U.S.A.

Ellie Darkins spent her formative years devouring romance novels and, after completing her English degree, decided to make a living from her love of books. As a writer and editor, she finds her work now entails dreaming up romantic proposals, hot dates with alpha males and trips to the past with dashing heroes. When she's not working, she can usually be found running around after her toddler, volunteering at her local library or escaping all the above with a good book and a vanilla latte.

Books by Ellie Darkins

Harlequin Romance

Newborn on Her Doorstep
Holiday with the Mystery Italian
Falling for the Rebel Princess
Conveniently Engaged to the Boss
Surprise Baby for the Heir
Falling Again for Her Island Fling
Reunited by the Tycoon's Twins
Snowbound at the Manor
From Best Friend to Fiancée
Prince's Christmas Baby Surprise

Visit the Author Profile page at Harlequin.com.

For Charlie, Loobie, Rosie and Harry

CHAPTER ONE

'WHAT ARE YOU doing here?' Jonathan asked, his heart stuttering as he realised who had just walked into his house. He couldn't be the only one who could hear his voice was so strained that it was starting to crack, but how else was he meant to sound when he was faced with the woman he'd been thinking about but hadn't seen for the last seven years.

Rowan stared at him, looking as shocked to see him as he was to see her. He'd had barely more than glimpses of her since then—anything more direct than a sideways glance would have risked a flood of emotions he'd never trusted himself to examine, for fear of what he might learn.

A few minutes ago, his sister, Liv, had walked into the house—a small manor in the Cotswolds that he'd inherited from his grandparents a few years back, and was getting ready to sell—without a word of explanation as to why her best friend was there. Then she'd walked straight up the stairs, leaving him and Rowan in the hallway, staring at each other.

'Livia invited me,' Rowan said, falteringly, and Jonathan would have given every penny in his bank account to know what she was thinking at that moment. 'I had no idea you'd be here, or I wouldn't have come. I'm sorry, I think I can still make the last train back to London if I hurry.'

He couldn't take his eyes off Rowan, who was staring him down in equal shock. He was distracted by a flashback of the last time that he had seen her and— No. He couldn't. He'd forced himself not to think about that night. It was the only thing that had stopped him from doing something stupid. He wasn't about to change that now.

He checked his watch. 'No, you'll have missed it,' he said with a sigh. 'God forbid Liv would check with me before inviting you.'

That made her look directly at him at last. 'Is it really so terrible that I'm here?'

Jonathan sighed, because of course it wasn't, and it was. It was torture, and it was wonderful. But he couldn't tell Rowan any of that. He couldn't let himself think that. He had to shut down his thoughts before they could lead him in a direction he couldn't afford to follow.

'The roof's leaking,' he blurted, and Rowan widened her eyes. 'None of the rooms on the second floor are habitable. I cleared a room each for Liv and Caleb but there isn't a spare.'

Rowan fixed him with a look. 'I'll share with Liv.'

Jonathan nodded. 'Yes. Right. Of course.' *Why* had he had to bring up sleeping arrangements? He should never, *never* be allowed to think of Rowan and beds together. He'd drive himself insane.

Livia called from the top of the stairs, and Rowan shouted up that she'd be there in a minute. 'Well, Jonathan,' Rowan said in an impressively cool voice that made him hope that she'd forgotten what had happened between them, and that perhaps he could just pretend that he had too.

'It's been such a long time,' he blurted out,

and nearly slapped a hand over his mouth to stop himself making it worse. Why had he said that? When he could have turned on his heel, retreated to the library and avoided her until she left. Bringing up the last time he had seen her was the very last thing he should be doing.

'Seven years,' Rowan said, with crossed arms and a raised eyebrow that told him that his luck was out and she remembered exactly the things that he had said back then. 'I have a race at the weekend and Liv is going to be my support crew,' she went on, putting him out of his misery. He could only be thankful for her mercy, because she'd somehow dissolved every defence mechanism that he'd honed over the years just by appearing in front of him. 'She promised me a few days of R&R here first. If I'd known that this was a family thing...'

'Right. Of course,' he replied. 'It is. Caleb's here too. I asked them to come and see if there was anything they wanted to keep before the estate agent comes next week. I... er...' He hesitated, not sure why he was explaining all this. Not entirely sure why she was staying to listen to him. 'I have a lot of work to do,' he added, hating how stuffy that sounded. As if he were a professor of hers, or a grandparent, rather than a man a scant few years older than her who once considered himself her friend. And had… Well, the less he thought about that the better.

'Far be it from me to keep you,' Rowan retorted, and he supposed that he deserved that. He knew that he sounded like a prig, but around Rowan, more than anyone, he couldn't afford to let his guard down. She would be so easy to love. Perhaps if he wasn't quite so aware of that, he could let himself…like her a little more? Could enjoy her being in his life in a peripheral sort of way. But he knew how dangerous that would be. Knew that spending time with her led to wanting her, led to…

He couldn't afford to love her. To love anyone else.

He already loved his family. He loved his job—as head of the business his grandparents and parents had left to him. And the responsibilities that came with them ate up every last shred of energy and reserves that he possessed. There simply wasn't space in his life for him to love anyone or anything else.

When it came to Rowan, he knew that he had to be careful. Because he hadn't guarded himself as well as he should have when they were friends, and it had led exactly where he knew that he couldn't go. Was it lonely, knowing that he was never going to have the thing that he knew he would want, if he allowed himself to be selfish? Of course it was. Some days, it had been so lonely that he hadn't been able to bear it.

But that was a small price to pay. Because he knew that the alternative was hurting the people he loved. He simply couldn't picture a life where he had the time and commitment he would want to give a loving, committed relationship. And so he had decided that that simply couldn't happen for him. He had kept his distance from Rowan and tried to forget her.

His entire adult life had been one carefully considered decision after another—balancing his responsibilities, parsing out his attention where it was needed most. He had protected his family and their business for every minute of the ten years since his parents had decided that they would be happier living in a South American country than facing the consequences of their unorthodox financial arrangements and the enormous bill the HMRC had landed on their doorstep.

No, they had left it to him to try and dig their family company—Kinley, a prestige brand in British fashion for more than a century—out of the financial and legal hole that they had created, not to mention the welfare of his siblings, then at university and boarding school. He'd kept the business afloat, just about. And his siblings? That had fared about as well. Not a great flaming tragedy—yet. But not something that he could look upon with any sense of pride or finality.

It seemed that he had failed, miserably, at the one thing that gave him any chance of protecting his heart. Rowan had been impossible to forget, and that was even before she had turned up on his doorstep. Just like that, all those years of effort had been washed away.

'I guess I'll see you, then,' Rowan said, turning and walking up the stairs without a backward glance.

Jonathan stared after her, praying that she wouldn't turn back and catch him. He shouldn't watch her. Had no right to look at her, and yet he couldn't help himself.

He was going to kill Livia.

CHAPTER TWO

How was Jonathan in the hallway *again*? Rowan asked herself as she came downstairs later that evening.

'Liv's having a shower so I'm going for a walk before dinner,' she threw out there, pointedly not inviting him just so that he would know that she wasn't seeking him out. That was the last thing that she wanted. She would never admit it, but she had been hiding in their room since she had arrived, and the claustrophobia was making it hard to breathe. She just wanted some fresh air, and this far out into the Cotswolds, that basically meant walking or running. She was meant to be resting her legs this week—with a hundred miles to run on Saturday she had to think carefully about every step that she took—but there was no way that she could be cooped up inside the house until then.

Maybe she should have followed her first instinct and booked herself on the first train back to London in the morning. She could make her own way back and find an Airbnb for the night before the race.

She walked through to the boot room to find the walking boots that Liv had promised should be in there and tried not to notice Jonathan's footsteps following her. It took every shred of resolve she had not to turn to him. She felt his presence all over her skin, a flush of shame and embarrassment. The worst part of it all was the fact that he still had this effect on her. That seven years after she had last seen him she could still feel his lips against her skin. Feel the way that she had showed him exactly how she felt about him and he couldn't have pushed her away harder if he'd been actively trying to break her heart.

'Rowan, can I have a word?' he said quietly.

'Don't,' she whispered, glancing over her shoulder to make sure that Liv and Caleb weren't about to sneak up on them. The only thing that could make his rejection of her worse would be if other people found out about it, and she could no longer pretend to herself and the whole world that it had never happened. 'It's ancient history,' she added, hoping that she could at least make him believe that she felt that way. She didn't need to pick the scab over that memory any more than she already had.

That was fine. Perfect. There had been a time that she would have teased him about being stuffy and tried to ease some of the atmosphere between him and Livia. When a half-smile from him would sustain her heart for days. She'd always thought that she'd had a way of reading Jonathan, a way of seeing him, that was different from his family. When he'd been pitched into the position of *de facto* parent to Liv, her best friend had seemed to see it as a challenge to relive her rebellious teenage years. Without complicated family dynamics, her relationship with Jonathan had been simpler. She'd always been able to tease a good mood from him, even when the pressure of his new responsibilities had weighed heavy in the crease of Jonathan's forehead and the new curve of his shoulders as he sat at his desk in the London family home.

She had thought of it as a kindness, at first, to try and cheer him up when Liv was always giving him a hard time. But the reward of each smile grew larger, and she challenged herself to win a grin, a chuckle, a laugh. And by the time she had done all that, she couldn't pretend to herself that she wasn't doing it for herself too. That she didn't get a flush of satisfaction knowing that she could reach him when everyone else received a scowl just for darkening his door. Livia never tired of complaining about what a bear he was with her.

Rowan had thought that what they had was a friendship. That those chats they'd had, over the kettle, or from his office doorway while Liv had cued up a movie or taken a shower, were some of the most genuine, authentic conversations that she'd ever had. And she'd grown to look forward to them. To anticipate the nights that Livia suggested they hang out at her place with a movie rather than go out to a bar or a club. She never told her friend about her conversations with her brother, though. She knew that Livia would laugh at her. Jonathan was someone to ridicule, in her friend's eyes. Not someone to fancy. But God did she fancy him.

He was tall, lithe, sandy-haired. His beard was always as neat as his carefully ironed shirts. She never failed to wonder at that. His whole world had fallen apart, he'd been landed with responsibility for his family and the family business. And instead of drinking overly sweet cocktails and angry-kissing strangers in nightclubs—Livia's chosen coping mechanisms in times of distress—Jonathan had exerted exceptional levels of control over his business, his family and his appearance. Livia hadn't exactly thanked him for it, and in their younger years Rowan had had to bite her tongue and hide her true feelings about Jonathan.

Which meant that she'd never spoken to her best friend about the night when Rowan had decided to lean in to what had felt like a 'moment.'

She and Jonathan had found themselves alone of an evening, while Liv was stuck on a delayed train home, instead of at the movie and pizza night that they'd planned. So Rowan had ended up sharing a pizza and a bottle of wine with Jonathan instead.

But they hadn't got round to the movie. Instead, they'd found themselves talking on the sofa. For hours. The windows had grown dark while they chatted, and they'd moved closer and closer, at one point pulling a blanket across both of them when a chill had reached them. Looking back, she hadn't been able to work out how they had moved so close together. She knew that she hadn't done it on purpose. But at some point, her feet had found their way into Jonathan's lap. His arm had fallen over the back of the sofa and started playing with her hair. An hour later that same arm was around her shoulders, and she wasn't sure who leaned in first but their lips were brushing together, first gently and then with an urgency that she had never felt before.

Hands had wandered and Jonathan's mouth had explored her jaw, her throat, her collarbones. Somehow, she had found herself lying back, Jonathan between her thighs, her legs around his waist pulling him closer.

She hadn't had the brain function to properly think about where it had been going, all she'd known was that she'd had no intention of stopping. It was everything that she wanted, everything that she had been waiting for. Jonathan was everything that she'd wanted, she'd realised, as she pushed one hand into his hair and the other under his shirt.

But then he'd pulled away, panting, and where she'd expected to see her own desire reflected in his face there was only shock. Something that was terribly close to horror.

He'd apologised and pulled his clothes back into place and turned his back on her, while she'd sat up on the sofa, asking herself what had gone wrong, what *she'd* done wrong to put that expression on his face.

'I'm sorry, I shouldn't have…' he'd stammered. And then looked at the bottle of wine they'd been sharing and blanched. 'You've been drinking. You don't even know what you're doing. Oh, my God, you're barely more than a kid. I'm sorry, Rowan.'

She'd not waited to hear the specifics of what he was sorry about. She'd pulled her T-shirt down over her breasts, pushed her hair back into a ponytail and got out of there before the tears could start. It had been years since that humiliating night and she had been lulled into a false sense of security, believing that hers and Jonathan's paths simply wouldn't cross again.

She had told herself that Jonathan probably didn't even remember it. Probably didn't even remember *her*. But as soon as she'd seen him standing in the hallway, she realised how wrong she had been. Not only did he remember, he was still visibly cringing at her mistake. Never in her adult life had she felt as mortified as she did in the moment that he'd told her that she didn't know what she was doing. She'd realised as soon as Jonathan kissed her how long she'd been waiting and hoping for that to happen, that she'd not been able to admit it even to herself, because she'd never thought that it would happen. And then it had happened, and as soon as Jonathan's brain had caught up with his libido he'd blamed it on having had too much to drink and all but thrown her out.

She had been under the mistaken impression that she no longer knew how to burn with shame and self-loathing, but her mind was filled with the words that she'd heard over and over again at school: that she was a freak, that no one would ever fancy her. That no one would find a girl who was taller than him sexy. Words that had continued to echo long after she'd left the classroom behind.

She'd thought that the therapy she'd invested in handsomely over the years had undone the damage that a decade of school bullying had created. That had been proved laughably false as her face burned and hands shook, all while Jonathan regarded her with what could only be pity.

Well. That had been when she was just twenty-one, barely out of university. She was older now and she knew better. She knew she could look at Jonathan and feel nothing, except perhaps sympathy for the girl she had been, with her hang-ups and her insecurities about her body, and her secret tears over the teasing she had endured day in, day out at school. Which she'd thought Jonathan was above until he'd hurt her worst of all.

She could feel him standing behind her while she found Liv's walking boots and pulled them on, tugging hard on the laces.

'Rowan?'

She looked up at his earnest tone of voice, and tried to prevent herself melting just a little bit at the sight of his concern.

'I didn't know you would be here this week,' she told him. It seemed like the most important thing, for him to know that she hadn't intentionally crashed this family week. That she hadn't chosen to spend a week in a house with him. If it had been up to her, she wouldn't ever see him again. 'My race at the weekend starts a couple of miles away and Liv asked if I'd like to spend a few days here, and... I wouldn't have come if I'd known.'

'You don't have to avoid me,' he replied, with a coolness that made her shrink away from him. Because somehow she'd rather that Jonathan was avoiding her than indifferent: indifference from someone she'd once felt so *much* for was unbearable.

'I didn't say that I was avoiding you,' she rebutted him, childishly, because it had to be obvious to him that she had, of course, been avoiding him. And the reason why had to be entirely self-evident.

Jonathan pinched the bridge of his nose. Rowan got the feeling that he was finding this very trying, and she couldn't make herself feel sorry for it.

'Okay, we're not avoiding each other. And

we're not making an effort to see one another. We're just two people who exist independently in Livia's orbit.'

'That seems like an accurate assessment,' Rowan confirmed. She allowed herself a quick peek across at him, but looked away as soon as she realised he was watching her. 'Honestly, Jonathan, it's fine,' she lied with a resigned sigh. 'We're fine. If you were going to talk about what I think you were going to talk about, there's no need. I haven't thought about it for years before tonight. I just want some fresh air and to stretch my legs.'

Relief was evident in his face, and she tried not to be too hurt by the evidence that he was so keen that they both keep what had happened very much in the past. 'I'll probably get the train home in the morning anyway, so you won't have to worry about seeing me again. I mean, we made it seven years before this, maybe we won't ever see each other again after tonight.'

CHAPTER THREE

ROWAN HAD STOMPED around the grounds of the manor for an hour, trying to get Jonathan's face out of her mind. She was past this. She'd spent so much time and money trying to get him out of her head. Had been on so many dates to try and find someone who would make her forget him.

But nothing had worked. Yes, in time, she'd thought of him less. There were times when she'd met someone funny and cute and kind, and one date had turned into two had turned into three. And then when she'd taken the plunge and thought about sleeping with them, Jonathan's face had got stuck in her head, and somehow no one had quite measured up to the man who had broken her heart.

Which was how she had found herself as the last virgin in London, desperate to move on, but never quite getting there. Now here she was, stuck with him in a picture-perfect house in the countryside. As she'd walked around the gardens, an idea had started forming, one that she couldn't quite convince herself was completely terrible. All this time, she'd clung on to what had happened that night, to the way that Jonathan had rejected her. She'd let that rejection reinforce all the worst things that she'd ever heard or believed about herself. Trying to forget it—forget him—trying to pretend that Jonathan didn't exist, hadn't worked. So perhaps she needed to do something else to get past this.

What if she could have a do-over? A chance to do things on her terms this time: kiss him, have things end without her lying in a heap of shame and self-loathing, call it quits. Maybe then she could have some closure and move on. It had to be worth a shot—after all, nothing else had worked, and she couldn't stay hung up on him for ever.

When she'd finished exploring the gardens, she'd gone back upstairs to the room that she was sharing with Liv, her stomach rumbling, her mind buzzing with her new idea. With perfect timing Caleb had knocked at their bedroom door and asked if they wanted to order pizza.

Rowan had always had a soft spot for Caleb. He'd still been away at boarding school when his parents had done a bunk, and she'd never seen as much of him as she had of Livia and Jonathan. Now, as an adult, he was even more of a mystery. She'd never been exactly sure what his job was, only that it was something frighteningly clever with computers and there was almost certainly something to do with cryptocurrency, and she'd heard him speaking at least three different languages in Zoom calls since they'd arrived.

Liv and Rowan ordered their usual, and then heard a string of message alerts coming from Caleb's room and he looked behind him. 'Can someone go down and ask Jonathan if he wants anything while I deal with that?'

When she glanced across at Liv, her friend was making puppy-dog eyes, which could realistically only mean one thing. 'Will you do it? Please?' Liv and Jonathan's relationship had been strained ever since he'd been expected to take over the parenting role. They barely spoke now, unless Jonathan insisted on it, and Rowan had no desire for them to start arguing. It was probably best for everyone if they stayed out of one another's way this week.

Besides that, it was the perfect excuse to go and talk to him—work out if this ridiculous plan of hers was even going to be possible. There was no point in pinning all her hopes for moving on—on the chance of kissing him again—if he wasn't at all interested. She wasn't going to do this unless she was sure that he wanted to. And she wouldn't be able to find out if she was always hiding upstairs.

'Yeah, I'll go ask him,' she said, hoping that she was making it sound casual. She just had to know whether this idea of hers even stood a chance.

She made her way down the stairs and towards the library, because she knew without even having to think about it that that was where she would find Jonathan. Always in the room with the highest concentration of books. Here at the manor, it was the library, with its floor-to-ceiling bookshelves, sliding ladder and French doors where she could picture him looking moodily out at the gardens.

With just socks on her feet, she barely made a noise moving through the house, even on the scuffed old flagstones of the entrance hall. She realised how stealthy she had been when she reached the door of the library, to find Jonathan at the ocean-liner-sized desk. Head leaning on one hand, train track creases across his forehead and between his eyebrows.

His gaze was fixed on the laptop screen, and she saw his eyes moving steadily side to side as he concentrated on whatever it was he was reading. She allowed herself a moment to watch him, aware even as she did so that it was both foolish and self-indulgent. Any minute now he was going to look up, or Liv was going to appear behind her, and she would have to explain herself. But it had been so long since she'd let herself look. When they'd first met, she'd been too shy. Averting her eyes, her cheeks on fire any time they had been in the same room, no matter talking to one another. But as their friendship had progressed, she'd grown bolder, meeting his gaze and holding it while they talked. But that confidence to look at him as an equal had been shattered years ago, and now she had to take what she could get. Like spying on him from a doorway while he was working. She cleared her throat, breaking the silence so he'd have no reason to think she'd done anything but just walk up.

For a moment, just as he looked up, she'd been convinced that he'd been about to smile. But it couldn't have been more than a trick of the light, because it was gone by the time she had blinked.

'Yes?' he asked, shattering all her illusions of intimacy.

For a moment she nearly lost her nerve and escaped back upstairs. But she was here for a reason, and she wasn't going to let his rudeness put her off her goal. Now that she'd thought it, kissing him again seemed like the only way she was ever going to leave that disastrous evening behind her. She needed to do this. She *was* going to get over him, and then she *was* going to go the whole of the rest of her life without thinking about him ever again. 'Caleb's ordering pizza,' she said, in a voice that she hoped gave away none of the above. 'Do you want anything?'

'Caleb could have asked me himself,' Jonathan observed, and Rowan felt her heart plummet to somewhere around the floor. Could he really not bear to talk to her even to give her his pizza order? She kept her face smooth, as she had had to learn to do at school, so he couldn't see how much that affected her.

'He asked me to,' she said calmly, refusing to be hurt that he was pushing her away. She'd simply not let him. She knew how Jonathan built walls when he was stressed—which was always—and they'd crumbled for her before.

She couldn't quite believe that she was putting herself through this again, but if she didn't, what did she have to look forward to—a lifetime of comparing every man that she met to him, and never quite being satisfied?

'I wasn't planning on stopping for dinner,' he said, and she could see that he was itching to get back to whatever he was doing on his laptop. He needed to take a break, but nothing would make that less likely to happen than to point it out to him.

'I wasn't asking you to,' she said shortly, not trusting herself to say more.

He sighed and rubbed at his forehead. 'Fine. I can stop for half an hour,' he said, though she hadn't challenged him. 'Just order me whatever you're having.'

He glanced up at her, a touch of pink in his cheeks, and she wondered what he had been thinking. Her smile as she looked down at her phone was involuntary and entirely unwelcome. 'Food will be here in an hour,' she told him, and turned in the direction of the kitchen. She found the larder and the wine rack, poured herself a glass of red wine and sat at the table, seeing off a few emails on her phone while she sipped at it and waited for the pizza.

She was still sitting at the table when the doorbell rang. She walked into the hallway with her eyes fixed on her phone and walked straight into Jonathan as he exited the library.

'Oof, what are you—'

'I was going to get the—'

She stepped away from him, brushing

down her clothes and refusing to be embarrassed just because her chest had knocked accidentally against his. She was a grownup. A professional. She was an accountant, for goodness' sake. A woman who had decided what she wanted and was confident that she could get it. That's what she would tell herself, every day, until she believed it— or until Jonathan proved her right. Which, seven years of therapy later, would probably be easier.

She hadn't moved, she realised when the bell rang again, and nor had Jonathan. His hand had come to rest on her upper arm, to steady her, she supposed, though they were practically the same height and she wasn't prone to toppling over. But the weight and warmth of his hand on her arm was sparking heat through her whole body. She'd forgotten what it did to her when she was the sole focus of his attention, when he looked her in the eye and it felt like whatever else was happening in the world it didn't matter in that minute. That when their eyes met, it conjured up some dimension where only they existed, and the real world couldn't touch them. This was what had led her into so much trouble before, and she didn't know whether she should be pleased or terrified that that place still existed.

Her cheeks warmed as she waited for him to step back. But he didn't. Was he feeling this too? she wondered. Was he remembering how good it used to feel, when they looked at each other like this? When everything else fell away, and it was just this?

'Was that the door?' Liv asked from above them, where she had appeared at the top of the stairs.

Rowan stepped away from Jonathan with a start and moved quickly to the front door, before the delivery driver decided no one was home and disappeared with their dinner. Before Jonathan had a chance to guess at what she'd been thinking and feeling. 'Food's here,' she called up, her voice shaking slightly.

CHAPTER FOUR

ROWAN WASN'T A kid any more. He didn't know why that should be a surprise, given that she was the same age as Liv, whose birthday he remembered every year. With their parents absent and their grandparents dead, it was yet another thing that was his responsibility.

Somehow the change in Rowan still took him by surprise. She'd been the tallest woman he knew since he'd met her. As a young woman, those long limbs had given her an awkward air, and she'd seemed to want to keep her body as small as possible. But that had fallen away as they had become friends— and he was sure that they had been friends.

Had she seen the way that he had started to look at her, how his gaze had lingered on her hair, her long legs, the way that she smiled when they talked, and she was her most relaxed self?

Until the day it had all gone wrong. He cringed to think of it now, how close he had come to losing control, and all the ways that he could have hurt Rowan and himself if he hadn't come to his senses and put a stop to it when he had.

They had spent the whole evening together, that day. He couldn't even remember now what they'd talked about. He couldn't even remember where Liv was. He was just so pleased to see Rowan on her own, for once. They had spent hours together, laughing, mostly. And it had been the first time since his parents had left that he'd felt truly relaxed. Had been able to stop worrying about the business and Liv and Caleb and what the hell he was going to do about the financial black hole at the middle of it.

The freedom of just *not worrying* for a few hours must have gone to his head. He'd felt positively drunk on it. It had seemed like the most natural thing in the world that they had moved closer and closer together as the night had gone on. That when a strand of Rowan's hair had fallen by his hand on the back of the sofa that he'd picked it up and let it slide through his fingers. When he looked down and realised that he'd used the arm around her shoulders to bring her closer that he'd brush his lips across hers.

The first touch of her lips had been like a match to dry kindling. He'd been utterly consumed by it. He'd acted entirely on instinct, in a way that he hadn't allowed himself for years. And who knows how far he would have let it go if he hadn't caught sight of the empty wine bottle out of the corner of his eye as he was shifting to press Rowan deeper into the sofa cushions.

It had suddenly crashed into him, what a colossal mistake he was making. Because Rowan deserved so much more than he could give her. So much better than to make a decision like this when she was tipsy and not in possession of all of the facts. Because he knew without a doubt that he didn't have room in his life for a relationship. Not for the sort of relationship that he knew he would want with Rowan. The type where he would want to love her and cherish her and protect her. Every minute of his life was spent worrying about the people he loved. The business he needed to keep afloat. He couldn't spare a minute to loving anyone else without something—someone—else suffering.

She deserved someone who could take care of her. Not someone who would take advantage of her after a bottle of wine and not have any time for her in the morning.

And because he was an idiot who never missed an opportunity to make things worse, he'd said something about her not knowing what she was doing, something about how young she was, and she'd disappeared from his life since that day. He thought that he'd never see her again.

She looked so different now to the last time that he had seen her, and it was harder than ever to ignore how he felt about her.

She held herself differently: her shoulders pushed back, her spine straight, hands confidently on her hips. She was taking up space, unapologetically, and observing him impassively. He hardly recognised the woman who had once felt like one of his closest friends. She was undeniably beautiful. He had always thought so, objectively speaking. But there was something mesmerising about her now. How was he meant to sit across from her and eat pizza without talking to her, explaining himself? Without doing something incredibly stupid, like falling for her?

He scrubbed a hand over his face, leaning against the door frame of the library, where Rowan had been just a few moments before. Watching as Liv and Rowan chatted effortlessly as they carried the pizzas through to the kitchen. He couldn't remember the last time he'd spoken to anyone with the ease that he saw in their friendship. No, that wasn't true. He remembered exactly when he'd last had a conversation like that. With Rowan. Right before he'd ruined it.

She was beautiful, sitting across the table from him, her body all long lines and hard-won muscle. She moved with intention, like she was aware of every single fibre of her limbs, placing her feet deliberately as she walked. Crossing her ankles and tucking her feet under her chair. He wanted to hook them with his own. Pull them out where he could accidentally knock against them and get her attention.

They passed the pizza boxes around while the other three chatted and he knew that he should make conversation, but he couldn't think of what to say that wouldn't make things worse.

He shouldn't be thinking about Rowan. He should be thinking about work. He had told himself that he didn't have time to stop for dinner, and here he was, away from his desk, all because she was here. He didn't know how he was going to pay his employees next month, and he was wasting time eating pizza, all because he couldn't bear the thought that Rowan was so close and he couldn't see her.

He couldn't afford to be distracted like this. His parents and then his grandparents had made the business and the family his responsibility. And he couldn't put it all at risk again. It was the reason that he had had to push Rowan away that night.

He had spent days expending his mental energy on how to pay his staff's wages and his suppliers from a pot of money that did not equal the sum of those numbers. He had to be one hundred percent focused.

That was why he had always kept his relationships brief, casual and with like-minded people who were no more interested in commitment than he was. It could never be like that with Rowan. One of his fundamental rules in his love life was that he could walk away with no one hurt any time the business or the family demanded more of him. Even before anything had started, he knew that a relationship with Rowan could never end that way. She simply wasn't someone he could walk away from.

He glanced up at Rowan listening with interest to Caleb talking about his work, and he couldn't take his eyes off her, licking her fingers when they got greasy from the pizza. He didn't realise Liv was trying to get his attention until she waved her hand in front of his face.

'You spaced out,' she said, as he raised an eyebrow in her direction.

'Sorry. Was just thinking about work,' he lied, hoping that no one at the table realised the true direction his thoughts had taken. The last thing he needed was Liv knowing that he was crushing on her friend. Wait, was that what he was doing? He froze, with a slice of pizza halfway to his mouth. Was that what was going on here? Because he had spent years telling himself that he missed their friendship. But he was distinctly aware that he had just thought the word 'crush.' He glanced at Rowan, a little panicked, and felt a tug in his chest as she laughed, doing battle with a long thread of melted mozzarella.

Was this a crush? The way that he felt when he looked at Rowan? He tried to think about it logically. He had been surprised to see her here, but undoubtedly pleased, once the initial shock had burned away. His stomach had fallen when he'd realised how their conversation was getting away from him. How he'd thought of her just now when he'd been thinking about relationships. He felt suddenly cold. Because it seemed so obvious that he had a crush on Rowan. Somehow he couldn't understand how it had taken him so long to realise it. Of course you didn't keep thinking of someone for years since you'd last seen them just because she was your sister's friend who you'd kissed one time. She was special to him. Always had been.

He had to deal with this. Right, like it was that simple. It *had* to be that simple. Now that he had recognised these feelings for what they were, he would be better prepared to deal with them. He would keep his distance from her, bury this…interest…in her deep down and get through this week.

From the look on her face when he glanced up at her just now, she wasn't exactly glad to be in his company. All he had to do was stay out of her way.

'I want to explore some more tomorrow,' Rowan said, trying to bring him into the conversation. 'I'm going to see if the maze is still navigable. What are you planning on doing with your day?'

'I need to work,' he said, reflexively, knowing that the less time he spent with her the better for his peace of mind. He had spoken to her for barely ten minutes in total today, and he was already stopping work to have dinner and spacing out thinking about her. 'Any spare time I get needs to be spent sorting through Grandmother's study before we hand over the keys to the estate agent. I was going to ask Liv to do it, but I guess I'll have to now. There might be papers in there that need sending to the archives. I don't want to lose anything important.'

'Then don't sell the house?' Liv suggested from the other side of the table, with her eyes narrowed at him.

He tried not to let his irritation show. Liv had been pissed off with him since he had first told her that he was selling the manor. She had no idea that it was breaking his heart to do it, but he didn't have the funds to stop the place disintegrating around them. And he had no intention of leaving wages unpaid just so that they could keep hold of their country retreat. He was just glad that he and his siblings had inherited their properties from their grandparents separately. Liv had inherited a London town house and Caleb a villa on Lake Como. This way, he could sell off his assets and generate some cash without them having to know how dire things really were. He had no desire to burden her with that information. But it did make snidey asides like that one difficult to swallow.

Jonathan gritted his teeth. 'It's my house, and I'm selling it, Liv. If there's anything inside that you want to keep, you're welcome to it. But you're not going to change my mind.'

'Cut it out, you two,' Rowan interrupted, drawing both of their attention. 'Liv, I'm sure you didn't invite me here to be stuck in the middle of a family argument so let's change the subject.'

Even Caleb looked up on her, a surprised grin on his face. 'Nice one, Rowan.'

She shrugged. Jonathan knew that he was looking at her still, startled. He had never, ever heard Rowan raise her voice before, and he felt slightly shamed that he was the cause of it, and for squabbling with his little sister, no less.

She shouldn't have snapped at them, but she couldn't help it. They were all so…careless with one another. If she'd had siblings—default playmates and defenders and allies—maybe her childhood would have been easier. But she'd been an only child to quiet parents and hadn't made friends at school. Maybe she wouldn't have seen herself as such an easy target for the bullies if she'd had a sister at school with her; she could have fought back, knowing she would have someone to defend her. She'd mentioned the problems to her parents, her teachers, but they'd brushed it off as 'kids being kids' and she hadn't wanted to cause a fuss.

Her height had made her a visible target—

she'd been six feet tall by the time she was fifteen—and her loneliness had made her vulnerable. When she had arrived at university, still alone, terrified that her school experience was about to repeat itself, it was pure luck that she found herself sharing a flat with Liv, who turned out to be her platonic soulmate, looking for people to love in the absence of her parents, recently departed for South America. They'd both been studying at the business school—accountancy for Rowan, marketing for Liv—and it had been her first true friendship. Gradually, it had transformed her. It had been Liv who had taken her to her first yoga class, where she'd discovered for the first time the wondrous things her body could *do*. That it was so much more than the way it looked. And a friend from yoga who had taken her with her on a run for the first time, which was when she had discovered how it felt to challenge her body, and have it come through for her.

It was a work in progress. Running for half an hour—which had once felt impossible—had proved to her that she shouldn't prejudge what she was capable of. Over the course of the last few years, she'd pushed herself further and further, to the point where she'd finished a marathon and thought to herself, *Why not just keep going?* It was in ultra-endurance running—races of thirty miles, fifty and, in the last year, a hundred—that she had found the strength to still her mind and quiet the critical voices that sounded so much like her childhood tormentors.

But she hadn't had so much resilience the last time that she'd seen Jonathan, when he'd knocked her back and left her feeling like the stupid kid he obviously saw her as.

This wasn't the girl he remembered, Jonathan thought again, the one who had carried herself awkwardly, uncomfortable in her own body, whose voice he had had to strain to hear.

She had a confidence and a sureness that hadn't been there before, and he liked it. It wasn't even a conscious thought. Just something deep inside him that told him that he wanted more of this. More of her. He'd take more of being yelled at by her for squabbling with his sister if that was all she was offering, as long as it was *more. Except...* Except then his brain caught up with itself, and he realised his mistake. He couldn't *have* more. He couldn't even want it. There wasn't room in his life for 'more.' If he started something with Rowan, then what was going to slip? Would it be the business? His family? Both of those were only holding together by a thread. The business because he kept throwing his savings at the black hole the bank accounts had become. His family because they didn't know how bad things were.

He couldn't let himself want something that would distract him from keeping it all afloat. He'd been forced to take responsibility for it all when he was barely an adult and had been trying to do his best at it ever since. He'd made it the most important part of his life since he was twenty-eight, and even that was never enough.

CHAPTER FIVE

'WHAT THE HELL?' Jonathan muttered, the banging at the front door pulling his thoughts away from next month's financials for the first time in hours. Liv and Rowan had decided to go to the pub hours ago—Rowan had still been talking about getting a train back to London in the morning, and Liv trying to convince her to stay. He'd been at his desk ever since, moving numbers around in his spreadsheet in the hope that they would magically multiply. He glanced at the clock in the corner of the screen—half past eleven—and assumed that it must be Liv and Rowan back from the pub. But why the hell didn't Liv just use her key to get in? At the sound of another crash at the door, he pushed his chair back and walked across the hall to the front door. He opened it wide, and Liv and Rowan practically fell across the threshold.

'What the hell,' he asked again, wedging his shoulder under Liv's arm on instinct, taking her weight as Rowan struggled at her other side. 'What happened?' he asked, as Liv cried out in pain. He had assumed she was just drunk, but her expression was creased and tense, rather than the dreamy vacancy she got after a drink too many.

'Twisted my ankle,' Liv said through another hiss.

'She's broken it, I think,' Rowan said, stopping for a moment to catch her breath. 'We're probably going to have to get it looked at.'

'Are *you* okay?' Jonathan asked Rowan, catching her eye. She was grimacing too, and he knew that with a race coming up an injury would be devastating.

'I'm fine,' she said. 'Have just carried this one the best part of a mile, that's all.'

'Here, I've got her,' Jonathan said, wrapping an arm around Liv's waist and taking all her weight so that Rowan could take a break. Her face was lined around the eyes and she didn't look much better off than his sister did. He kept a watch on her in his peripheral vision, just to be sure that she was okay.

'How did it happen?' he asked, as he lowered Liv onto a bench on the other side of the hall and then looked around for his car keys. He turned to Rowan for an answer, since Liv was currently pressing her hands to her own face.

'We were walking back and she caught her foot in a foxhole,' Rowan said. 'I couldn't get a proper look in the dark, but it seems pretty swollen and she can't put any weight on it.'

'You should have called me,' he snapped, his tone sharper than he'd intended. He regretted it the moment he saw the hurt on Rowan's face. *This* was why he had wanted her to leave. Because it was impossible for him to be around people he cared about without hurting them. All he wanted to do was protect his family, and yet doing so left him so strained and stressed that it came out like *this*, angry and accusatory, when all he wanted to do was care.

He'd proved that the last time he'd spent any time with Rowan that he couldn't let his feelings for her show without hurting her. The last thing he wanted to do was repeat that.

'No signal,' she told him, sitting beside Liv and pulling her hands from her face. 'Doing okay under there?' she asked. Liv replied with a creased brow and pulled her hands back over her face.

'I'm sorry, I didn't mean to snap,' Jonathan said, catching Rowan's hand to get her attention, and then dropping it again when he realised what he'd done. 'I've got my keys,' he said, picking Liv back up. 'Can you get the doors if I carry her?'

'Rowan, come with us?' Liv asked over his shoulder, and he could hardly argue with his sister when she was in so much pain. Rowan told Caleb, who had appeared on the stairs, what was happening, and then led the way out to the car.

Once Liv had been X-rayed and a broken ankle diagnosed, and had been plastered and medicated and discharged, it was almost light outside. He'd driven home along the winding lanes, got his sister settled in bed and then found himself alongside Rowan in the kitchen, in the small hours of the morning, in a house that was silent apart from the distant rattle of water pipes as he filled the kettle.

'Tea?' Jonathan asked, because although what he really wanted was a whisky, he didn't trust himself to give up even a smidge of self-control around Rowan, not when he had hurt her before, and knew he could again. It had been a very long night with very little sleep, and he knew better than to test his self-control. He wondered what she'd been thinking that night, when he'd come so close to forgetting all of the reasons why he couldn't give in to everything that he wanted and kiss her like he did when he was dreaming, when he played out everything in his sleep that he couldn't have in his waking hours.

'Chamomile, if you have any,' Rowan asked with a sigh, dropping onto the bench by the oak table in the centre of the room and bringing him back to his senses. 'I don't want anything that's going to keep me awake.'

'Are you sure you're not hurt too? I wish you'd let the doctors check you over, especially with your race coming up,' Jonathan said, watching her with concern as he placed the kettle on the range, only dragging his eyes away from her to hunt for the tea she wanted. He didn't know how to care for her without hurting her, so he concentrated on making her tea, wishing she would read into it how much she and their friendship had meant to him, and how sorry he was that he had spoilt what they had by hurting her, even though he was hurting himself more.

He placed the mug in front of her, and hesitated, before she moved along the bench to make room for him. 'I'm fine, just tired.'

'Thank you,' he said, 'for helping her. You must be exhausted.'

'She's my friend,' Rowan said. 'Of course I was going to help her.' Well, that put him in his place. Reminding him that it didn't matter how grateful he was to her, none of this had been for him. It didn't tell him anything about what she felt for him. Or what she had felt for him once.

'You know she'll hate having to let me look after her,' Jonathan added, which was true. And also the perfect excuse for Rowan to have to stay, because despite her mentioning the first train back to London earlier, he couldn't imagine her leaving now, not when Liv was going to be off her feet for days, at least.

'You're probably right,' she said, with a despondent look that could only mean that she was thinking the same thing. 'The more you tell her to take it easy the more she'll want to resist.' Rowan smiled. 'I think you two bring out the worst in each other.'

Jonathan gave a sad, helpless laugh at Rowan's assessment of his relationship with his sister, the one that he'd worked so hard at for so long, and only seemed to make worse. 'I only ever want what's best for her,' he said, trying to keep the pain out of his voice.

Rowan shocked him, reaching out and touching his hand. 'I know,' she said, her voice soft. 'I know Liv doesn't always appreciate you looking out for her, but I can see that you do it because you care. She's lucky to have you.'

He snorted. It was a kind thought, but he knew his sister didn't consider herself lucky. And why should she, when she had lost their parents and been left with a clueless brother who only seemed capable of making her hate him. Did Rowan see that he had been protecting her too, when he'd stopped her from kissing him back? Or had she only resented his overprotectiveness, as Liv always had?

Rowan must have only just realised what she had done with her hand, because she looked at it as if it belonged to someone else, before snatching it away and tucking it under her thigh, where neither of them could see it. He could see as she realised that she had let her guard down and needed to raise her defences. He wished there was something he could do to stop the stiffening of her shoulders, the blankness that she painted over her face.

'Rowan,' he said at last. 'I think maybe we should talk properly about the last time that we saw one another. I'm afraid that I may have given you the impression that—'

'I thought there was an attraction there,' Rowan said, cutting him off gently. 'I was young and maybe I misread the signals. I don't think we need to go over it all again.'

'Rowan, you weren't wrong,' Jonathan said, his voice low.

* * *

She held his gaze while she tried to understand his meaning. She hadn't *imagined* that he was attracted to her. Then why had he—?

'It just wasn't a good—' he started again, and this time she held up a hand to stop him finishing his sentence. She didn't need to know which part of it was bad. The fact that she'd kissed him or the kiss itself, or perhaps just her. She'd had enough voices in her head over the years telling her which parts of herself she should hate, and she didn't want to add his into the mix. She'd worked hard over the years to resist the worst thoughts that she had about herself. To retrain her brain not to believe the insults that had been hurled her way through her adolescence and were so resistant to being unstuck.

She was meant to be trying to make him want to kiss her again, not reminding herself of all the ways she had been hurt before. This wasn't going to help her get over him. To stop thinking about him. To stop judging every man she met against how much she had wanted him. How good it had felt to be close to him.

His long fingers wrapped around her

wrist, and he lowered her hand, slowly, until he was holding it between them. Jonathan's words had hit somewhere deep and painful. He was attracted to her, then, but hadn't *wanted* her. It hadn't been enough. *She* hadn't been enough.

If she was going to change what those voices said, to move on from what had happened that night, she needed for them to stop talking about the past. See what there was between them now, if anything, and how she could use that to get on with her life. He let out a sigh that made her nervous, pulling her spine a little straighter to counter the deepest habit of trying to make herself disappear. 'I just want…' Jonathan said, glancing down at their joined hands, and only now seeming to realise what he had done. He took a deep breath. 'I would really like it if we could get back to how we were before. When we were friends.'

She forced herself to smile…because she could take that, for now. It was somewhere to start from. They *had* been friends, once. They had been easy with each other. And he hadn't denied that he had been attracted to her. She hadn't been wrong.

Whatever had gone wrong that night, it hadn't been because he didn't want her. The knowledge that she had been right about that settled something deep inside her. That even at twenty-one with no experience and eyes for only this man, she'd been right when she'd known how he looked at her.

With that knowledge, her instincts for how Jonathan might feel about her now suddenly felt that little bit surer. Her plan to kiss him and move on that little bit more achievable.

'I'd like that,' she said. 'I hate how awkward things have been. I miss how it used to be.'

She pulled her hand gently away from him and then looked up to meet his eye. 'Okay,' he said, his expression warm, reminding her of when they'd been friends and she'd managed to convince herself that he wanted more. 'Friends.'

She wondered if he could hear all the things she was trying so hard not to say. Whatever else had gone wrong that night, she clung to that grain of certainty that Jonathan had given her. Because she wanted to know that she could trust her judgement. That when she caught him looking at her the way he had been tonight, she wasn't imagining the heat she saw in his eyes.

He had used the past tense before: *'Rowan, you weren't wrong.'* Did that translate into the present? Did he still find her attractive? Would he kiss her again?

She watched him watching her. His eyes rested on her face now, but she'd seen the way that they'd swept up and then down her body, lingering, before he'd realised she was watching him. She couldn't seem to shake the idea that she'd had in the garden earlier: what if she had the opportunity to finish what they'd started. Then could she stop carrying round this embarrassing torch for him? The one that seemed to get in the way of her forming something meaningful with anyone who wasn't him.

They were going to be thrown together more than ever now that Liv was stuck in bed with her ankle in plaster. And there wasn't any possibility of her going back to London tomorrow, as she'd thought about doing when she'd realised that Jonathan was at the manor.

'It's late,' she said, picking up her mug of tea and standing, knowing that she should at least sleep on this idea of hers before she did something that couldn't be taken back. 'Or early. Either way I should get to bed.'

Jonathan smiled, stood up at the same time as she did. 'So, I'll see you in the morning? Later in the morning, I mean.'

'Yeah. I'll be here. Liv will need me,' she said simply. Jonathan breathed a sigh.

'Then I'll see you later,' he said to her back as she walked from the room.

CHAPTER SIX

'How's Liv?' Jonathan asked Rowan as she walked into the kitchen after she'd finally managed a few hours of sleep. He was sitting at the table, laptop in front of him, and looking like he hadn't slept at all. She resisted the urge to pull the computer from him and send him off to bed.

Rowan gave him a grim smile. 'She's a trooper but needs some more pain meds. I'll make her some lunch to have with them. Do you want anything?'

'How about I make the bagels and you make the coffee,' Jonathan said, stretching his arms over his head as he got up from the table and then holding his hand out for the bread knife she'd picked up. Rowan looked down at his palm for a moment, enjoying the way he was reaching out for her. And handed over the knife, shivering when her fingers brushed against his. He glanced up at her, met her eye for a fraction of a second. Was that…something? He'd certainly seemed affected by it. But it was impossible to know whether it was in a good way or bad. She was careful how she moved around him as they buttered bagels and frothed milk and brewed coffee. Eventually, she had a tray heavily laden for her and Liv, and Jonathan leaned back against the worktop.

'You're sure you don't want me to carry that upstairs for you?' he asked. She knew Liv would have rolled her eyes and sighed, unable to see his desire to help as anything other than a desire to control her.

'It's fine,' she said with a careful smile. 'I've got it.' Jonathan nodded, and she knew that he was reining in his habitual need to insist, something he seemed quite capable of doing with her, but found impossible with his little sister.

She climbed the stairs easily, passed the click-clack sound of a keyboard coming from Caleb's room and pushed the door to her and Liv's room open with her shoulder. Only to be greeted by the sound of Liv's deep, resonant snores. Rowan had been grateful, in the end, to escape that sound by getting a couple of hours' sleep on the sofa in the family room—the only option left to her given that all the other bedrooms were damp and leaking. Even so, it had been draughty in there with the fire burned out, and the antique couch not exactly comfortable.

She left the tray on a side table, picked up her mug and plate and tiptoed out of the room. Liv had slept badly last night, and all her energy was going into healing her ankle. She'd wake when she needed her meds—there was no reason to disturb her before then. Rowan headed downstairs, wondering whether she would find the kitchen empty. But Jonathan was still in there, his long, lean form leaning against the counter with an ease she was sure she'd never achieve, regardless of how much yoga she did. She pulled herself up and reminded herself of the principle of non-violence—which applied just as much to oneself as it did to others. She needed to remember that accepting her body was an active choice; it would be all too easy to fall back into old habits.

Jonathan raised an eyebrow—presumably at her being back so soon.

'Liv was asleep,' she explained, taking a seat at the kitchen table and sipping her coffee. 'Noisily,' she added with a smile. 'There's no way I'm sharing a bed with her tonight.'

Jonathan choked briefly on his bagel. 'You're still planning on leaving?' he asked, banging his chest with a fist to dislodge the bagel.

Rowan narrowed her eyes at him. 'I only meant our room. I don't know if it was the meds or what but her snoring was ridiculous. I only managed to drop off once I gave up and moved to the family room for a couple of hours.'

'But you can't sleep there all night,' Jonathan declared in an authoritative tone that made her bristle. She didn't need to be made to feel like a stupid kid. Least of all by him.

'Why not?' she asked, folding her arms across her chest and glaring at him.

'Because it can't possibly be comfortable, for a start,' Jonathan said. 'Perhaps if you were Liv's height.'

She glared harder. 'Well, there's not much I can do about that.'

Jonathan looked a little surprised by her tone and held out his hands in a gesture of conciliation. 'I just meant you can't be comfortable there.'

'Well, I'm not sharing with Liv, and all the other rooms are taken. It's only a few days,' she said with a shrug.

'Take my bed,' Jonathan said, and she could see that he had surprised himself. Well, as if he was surprised, then remembered the way that he thought everyone's problems were his to solve and refused to accept that he didn't have to take responsibility for every single person he met.

'You don't need to worry about this, Jonathan. About me, I mean. If there aren't enough beds to go around, then someone has to take the sofa and I don't mind. I'm not taking your bed.'

'I can share with Caleb,' Jonathan countered, a hand rubbing at the back of his neck, and she wondered if he was regretting his offer already. And then she reached for her bagel and her back twinged, reminding her that he'd been entirely right—as annoying as that may be—and as long as he wasn't proposing to be in the bed himself, she had no real reason to turn down his suggestion. She only wished that he could see that not every problem was his to solve. He'd demanded that he be allowed to rescue her, without any thought about himself—not the first time over the years that she had noticed this tendency. It didn't take a genius to know that that wasn't the sort of thing you could keep up for ever. Sooner or later, you had to take care of yourself if you didn't want to burn out.

'I'm not sure about this,' she said gently. 'Why don't you think about it. I won't be upset if you change your mind.' But she knew there was little chance of that. Once Jonathan had decided you needed his protection, there was very little you could do about it.

'I absolutely insist,' he said, proving her point.

'Then I suppose I accept,' Rowan said, thinking of her plan to make him want her, and that this wasn't exactly how she had hoped to end up in his bed. But if she was going to be there, maybe it could work in her favour, somehow. This week was the longest time that she had spent with him for years. But all things considered it still wasn't actually all that long. If she was going to make him want her, she had to make a start soon.

And that start really had to be not leaving a room every time that Jonathan walked into one, so she fought down her instinct to go hide somewhere, and instead sipped her coffee as if she was perfectly at ease in his presence. The friends that they had decided to be, but which didn't seem quite natural yet.

'I need to make a start sorting through the papers in the library,' Jonathan said when he finished his tea, rinsing out his cup and leaving it on the draining board. 'There are decades' worth of loose sheets shoved into boxes and no one's looked at them for years. I'd like to be sure we're not throwing away anything that should be in an archive somewhere before we get rid of it all. Liv was going to help but...'

'Well, let me,' Rowan said, thinking that this was the perfect opportunity to be close to him for a while.

'You really don't have to,' Jonathan said with a frown.

'I've genuinely got nothing else to do,' she

said. 'I'm meant to be taking things easy, hanging out with Liv and resting up before Saturday. But if this morning is anything to go by she's going to be sleeping for most of the next few days. It'll be good to have something to do.'

He looked at her carefully, the narrowing of his eyes giving away his discomfort at the thought. But eventually he agreed, and she tried to hide how pleased she was.

So, they spent the morning together in the musty-smelling library, the French doors flung open to let in the sunshine and fresh air. The stacked cardboard boxes were treasure troves of ephemera, receipts and sketches and invoices going back to the thirties. She organised them by decade, first, holding up anything that she found interesting so that she and Jonathan could look at it together.

'You know you really don't have to do this,' Jonathan said from behind the desk, after they'd been working solidly for a couple of hours. He scratched his hands through his hair while his attention moved between the pile of papers in front of him and the laptop perched on a larger pile to one side.

'I already told you. I'm happy doing it,' Rowan told him. 'There's so much interesting stuff in here. It's like a puzzle. You know accountants love boxes of old receipts.'

He smiled, and she considered that a small victory. 'We should at least make Caleb help, though,' he added.

She shrugged, because she was happy that it was just the two of them in there. Somehow, sitting in silence had brought back some ease into their relationship, and she didn't want to risk the tiny steps they had taken back to normality, and towards whatever might come after that. 'Caleb seems pretty happy upstairs. And I like that there's someone near to Liv in case I don't hear her when she wakes.'

Jonathan smiled at that. 'I thought I was the one who was meant to be overprotective.'

She gave him a searching look. 'You don't get a monopoly over caring for her,' Rowan said, coming to stand by the desk, leaning and resting a hip against it. 'You don't have to be the only one who's allowed to.'

'She's my sister,' he pointed out, as if that explained everything.

Rowan thought for a moment, trying to understand the things that he wasn't saying, as well as the things that he was. She'd always loved that about him. How deeply he thought. How deeply he felt. Jonathan didn't know how to take things lightly, and that was a gift, and also—she imagined—deeply painful at times. 'I know that,' she told him. 'And you had to be more than a brother to her when you were way too young for that sort of responsibility. I'm not pretending to know how hard that must have been for you. But I wanted you to know you're not the only one who loves her. It's not all on you, you know.'

Jonathan sighed, as if he'd worked out where this was going, and didn't want to hear the rest of it. 'Thank you for saying that. It's not the same, but I appreciate it anyway.'

She looked at him for a few long moments, wondering whether to let him off the hook. Why it was so important to her that she made him understand that he wasn't alone in this one thing. 'Okay. Whatever you say,' she conceded at last. 'But let me carry on helping in here, at least,' she added. Jonathan nodded and shifted his laptop further to the side, scooting his chair back.

'Are you quite sure that the business doesn't explode when you do that?' Rowan asked with a grin.

He frowned, and she felt a twist of anxiety. She tried to laugh it off, but she couldn't help but feel like she'd touched something raw.

'It's okay, I'm just teasing. You deserve a break. When *was* the last time that you had a day off?' She saw his expression close off and reached out a hand to touch him gently on the shoulder. 'I'm not criticising,' she said, because he seemed not to believe her. 'I'm just concerned. Who worries about you while you're looking after everyone else?'

'I don't need worrying about,' he said, turning away from the desk and walking over to the pile of papers she'd been sorting through. She took that as a less than subtle hint that she wasn't going to get any further asking him about that. The last thing that he needed was to start worrying about the fact that Rowan might be worrying about him.

'So, how have you organised these?' he asked, looking through the boxes she'd made a start on.

'I've started chronologically,' Rowan said, flicking through the pile of papers closest to her. 'I don't understand why these aren't already in an archive somewhere,' she added.

'Because ever since I took over the business, I've been more interested in Kinley surviving the year than looking at cuttings from a century ago,' Jonathan said sharply.

'Hey, it wasn't a criticism,' she said, taken aback by his tone. She'd thought that Kinley's financial problems were all in the past. But the way that Jonathan phrased that made it sound very much like they were ongoing. That would go some way to explaining why it looked like Jonathan hadn't had a good night's sleep in months, if not years. 'Jonathan, are things…okay? With the business, I mean.'

'Of course. They're fine,' he said, before letting out a sigh that told her way more than those four words could.

'Because you know that I can help, don't you? Accountant, remember. If you want me to, you only have to ask.'

'You can't tell Liv,' Jonathan said, the words bursting out of him, seemingly against his will. Rowan sat back on her heels and looked at him closely. So, there was something to tell. She thought for a moment about her friendship with Liv, which had never had any secrets…other than the fairly whopping matter of having nearly slept with Jonathan all those years ago. Compared to that, helping him with his finances didn't seem so bad.

'I won't tell her if you don't want me to,' Rowan reassured him. 'Just tell me what's going on. Please. I want to help if I can.'

Jonathan rubbed his face in both his hands, and for a moment she wasn't sure if he was even going to look up again. Eventually, though, he dragged his gaze to meet hers, and her heart ached for the sorrow that she saw in his expression.

'There's no money, Rowan. None. That's what's going on. There has never been any money. And I've been trying to keep the business afloat by papering over the cracks and using my own savings and inheritance to fill the gaps. But now that's all gone and the accounts are still a black hole. I'm looking at a bill for a supplier that is already a month overdue and wondering how I can pay that and the wages and how a fashion house can survive with either no fabric or no staff. Is that the sort of thing you can help me with?'

Rowan took a deep breath and forced herself not to show on her face how much she agreed with him that actually that did sound pretty awful. She would get to that.

'Right...that's a lot. Jonathan. And don't snap at me for asking, but...why aren't we telling Liv about this? You all have shares in the business, right?'

But Jonathan shook his head, his face haunted. 'It's my responsibility to fix this. She shouldn't have to worry about this mess.'

Rowan frowned, her heart feeling soft around the edges. She forced herself to toughen it up. This wasn't about her feelings for Jonathan. She would look at the business side of things objectively in a minute. But she hated seeing him like this, like he had dug this hole himself and wasn't allowed to ask for help to get out. He wasn't responsible for the financial mess that they were in. That had been dumped on his shoulders with far too many other responsibilities when he was too young to be expected to carry it.

She could murder his parents for what they'd put him through. What they'd put them all through.

'You don't have to do it all alone, Jonathan. It's too much for one person. And, you know, Liv's a grown-up. She doesn't need you to be her dad. She could be on your side if you let her.'

'Please don't tell me what my sister needs. It's my job to worry about this.'

Rowan reached for his hands, because it seemed like nothing short of physical touch was going to get him to pay attention to what she was saying. And for reasons that she probably shouldn't examine too closely, it was suddenly imperative that she make him feel better. 'It's only your job because your parents left and heaped everything on your shoulders while the others were just kids. But they're as old now as you were then. Perhaps it's time to stop insisting on doing this all by yourself.'

The silence stretched out into long seconds, long enough that she wondered whether she might actually have got through to him. That he might be coming around to what she was saying. But then his face shuttered, and she knew that she'd failed. 'I'm not discussing this, Rowan. If you're going to help me, I need to know that I can trust you not to tell Livia.'

Rowan sighed, because she really did hate keeping secrets. But she could see from the expression on Jonathan's face how serious this was. There was really never any doubt that she would help him if he asked, regardless of what conditions he put on accepting her help.

'Okay, I'll help, and I won't say anything to Liv. If you'll promise me you'll think about sharing this with your family. Letting them help you with something for a change.'

'Fine. I'll think about it,' he said, though she suspected that he had no intention of changing his mind. She could work with that.

'Let's pack away some of these boxes and make some space at the desk. Maybe Liv can go through the boxes for archiving if she's up to it later,' Rowan said. 'Then we can go through your financials together and see where we are.'

Once the desk was clear, she pulled Jonathan's laptop in front of them both, and asked him to walk her through the most recent years' financial statements. Afterwards, she whistled through her teeth, not sure what she could say that wouldn't sound dramatic. 'You're right. It's not…good.' She heard a snort beside her, and when she looked round, couldn't believe what she was seeing. Jonathan was laughing. *Laughing!*

She hit him playfully on the arm. 'Don't laugh at me.'

'I'm not laughing *at* you,' he said, laughing so hard she was sure that she could see tears about to fall from his blond eyelashes. 'My brain is just… I'm fairly sure that I'm exhausted. "Not good" just pushed me over the edge.'

'Have you had a break at all today?' she asked, trying to give him a stern look. 'Have you even stepped foot outside?'

'I'm fine,' he told her, while refusing to make eye contact.

But he wasn't. That was clear to anyone remotely interested in looking. His face was pale, there were black bags under his eyes and creases at the corners where he'd been squinting too long at the screen. 'Come on, that's it,' she declared. 'I'm staging an intervention. You need fresh air and vitamin D.'

'I'm too busy,' Jonathan said, reaching for his laptop again before she caught him by the wrist.

'You're busy being a bore.'

That got a smile out of him, though he tried to hide it. 'Go outside yourself,' he said, his voice gruff.

Rowan hid a smile. 'You're aware that I'm the one helping you, yes?'

He sighed, pinched the bridge of his nose, and she was almost tempted to laugh in relief at the sight of that familiar gesture from him. 'Very aware,' he said, with something of a despairing tone.

'Seriously, though, it's so lovely out there. I know that there are some beautiful walks around here. Show me one of them. Show me the maze.'

He snorted. 'You don't need a chaperone.'

She tried not to let him see the moment when her face fell, before she hid the expression with her usual smile.

'Well, don't complain later that I didn't try and save you from your sedentary lifestyle,' she said with a careful shrug, straightening up some pages on the desk to cover her embarrassment. Jonathan sighed, and Rowan looked over at him.

'I'll come,' he said.

She was torn between wrapping her arms round him and stomping off in a huff at how pained he seemed to find the idea of both an hour off work and an hour spent with her. In the end, she decided that the middle ground was probably safest and only nodded.

'Great. Will you check in on Liv for me before we go? She'll snap at you because she's grouchy when she's in pain but she won't mean it.'

The warmth of the sun was so beautiful on her shoulders when she stepped outside that she worked her way through a couple of salutations, feeling them warm her body and giving her legs a gentle stretch. She turned when she heard Jonathan's footsteps on the gravel path that circled the house.

'Which way do you want to go?' he asked, and she wasn't sure if it was just an effect of the golden sunshine reflecting off the honeyed stone of the manor house, but he had lost some of his pallor already. His skin looked warm and golden, and he had lost that grey tone that had worried her in the library.

'Can we explore the maze?' Rowan asked. The path loped through the formal gardens behind the house, through a little overgrown thicket of trees and into a glade where the sunlight pricked sweat on her skin and made her wish she'd put on sunglasses before she'd left. She stopped to take a drink from the water bottle she'd thrown into her backpack.

'It's so pretty out here,' she said, as Jonathan stretched his arms above his head, no doubt pulling out all the knots that were inevitable if you spent sixteen hours a day in front of a computer. It made it difficult not to objectify him in a way that she knew was frankly rude—history or no history. That being said, she had rather been hoping that he might be looking at her in a similar way. He had said, out loud with no obfuscations, that he had been attracted to her. Though they had been talking very much about the past and not the present. But she really, really wanted not to think about him any more. Not without it leading anywhere. And the only way that she could think that she could possibly move on from him would be to do what they had stopped at the last moment. The only problem was, she had no idea how to get them from this point to there.

'Aren't you going for a run today?' Jonathan asked as they approached the old entrance to the maze, which had grown high and unruly above the once carefully tended yew trees. 'I assumed you went out every day.'

'Usually I do,' Rowan agreed. 'But not the week before a race.' She pushed aside the branches to reveal what remained of the path into the maze. It looked a little spooky in there, and all of a sudden she wasn't sure that this had been a good idea. 'I'll probably only do one short run this week. I want my legs fresh for Saturday,' she said in a carefully even voice, not wanting to let her hesitation show.

'Changed your mind about exploring?' Jonathan asked from close behind her. Far closer than she'd realised that he was standing. His breath tickled the hairs on the back of her neck, and she turned her head suddenly, only to find his face a scant inch or so from her own.

'No,' she said on impulse, because she didn't want him to think that she was so easily spooked. She was an adult. Something that he had somehow failed to recognise before, and she was going to make sure that he knew it now. Anyway, she wasn't sure *exactly* how abandoned mazes fit into planned seductions—having never been in one, or indeed seduced anyone before. But it didn't seem like a bad place to start.

She pushed aside the branches again and squeezed into the maze.

The interior was less overgrown, the height of the trees blocking out most of the sunlight. But it was still narrow enough that they had to walk single file and when she stopped abruptly for Jonathan's chest to hit her back before he had a chance to stop himself.

'Sorry,' he said, jumping back. She wondered whether she was supposed to tell him he had nothing to apologise for. That she didn't mind having his body pressed against hers. But they hadn't even made their first turn in the maze yet, and she didn't fancy being trapped in here if such an obvious come-on resulted in him rejecting her. Again. She'd wait until they were in the open before she offered her heart—no, her ego— up to be broken.

She remembered the thought that had made her stop so suddenly.

'Do you know the route to the centre?' she asked.

'That would be telling,' Jonathan replied, and even without looking round at him she knew that he was smiling.

'That was rather the point of me asking.'

He laughed, a sound that she took as a personal victory. 'There's no fun if I tell you the way,' he said.

'Aha! So you *do* know.'

'I've been coming here since before I can remember. Of course I know the way.'

'Won't you miss it?' Rowan asked, and even before Jonathan's hissed-in breath knew that she'd said the wrong thing.

'Of course I'll miss it,' Jonathan said, his voice low and creaky. She felt his sadness in her chest. 'This whole place feels like a part of me,' he went on. 'Like I'm a part of it. But there's not enough money to even stop it falling down, never mind do anything else with it. And I don't know if you realise this but I do actually need the money from selling this place to stop the Kinley business from completely imploding.'

They stood in silence for a moment, Rowan holding her breath, cursing herself for having said something so insensitive.

'I'm sorry—' they both said at once, and Rowan turned on the spot. It didn't matter how close they were standing, only that Jonathan knew that she hadn't meant to hurt him, or mock him, or taunt him. Or the hundred other ways that she knew her words could have hurt him.

'No, I'm sorry,' Jonathan said. 'I shouldn't have snapped. None of this is your fault.'

She watched as he reached and plucked something from her hair.

'Leaf?' she asked, glancing upward.

'Cobweb.'

She squealed so loudly that she slammed a hand across her mouth to stifle the sound.

'Oh my God,' she said at last, still through her fingers. 'I didn't think this through.'

Jonathan smiled but resisted the obvious urge to laugh at her.

'It was only a very small one. I didn't imagine you'd be afraid of spiders.'

'No? What have you been imagining about me?' she asked. It was only once the words were out that she realised how suggestive they might have sounded. And she could have rushed to take them back, but instead she let them settle into the trees around them. Felt the heavy charge in the atmosphere, the sudden awareness of how her body seemed to be able to feel how close they were together. How easily they would be able to touch, if only one or the other of them would take that last, tiny step.

She really, really wanted to know if Jonathan had ever fantasised about her. What he thought of. What he might be tempted to play out in real life. But she was also aware that they were standing in the middle of what was most likely a spider-infested maze and with the best will in the world she probably wasn't going to be able to push that entirely from her mind.

'Turn back or keep going?' Jonathan asked, and she wondered if he had intended for that to be so obviously loaded with double meaning. She wasn't going to take any chances.

'Keep going.'

She tore her gaze away from his, turned and kept walking, taking first a right and then a left, meeting one dead end after another. After so many about turns that she couldn't be entirely sure they were even in the same county any more, never mind the same maze, she finally gave in and asked the question that she'd been fighting back.

'Okay, I give up. Can you lead the way to the centre?'

Jonathan laughed, giving her a slightly bemused look. 'I know the way from the *start*. I'm sorry to tell you that I have absolutely no idea where we are, never mind how to get to the middle from here.'

She glanced around them, feeling the branches of the trees closing in on them. 'Maybe we should head back to the entrance, then?'

Jonathan lifted his hands up in apology.

'I've got no better chance of finding that than I have of finding the centre. We could try and retrace our steps. Make all our mistakes in reverse.'

She made herself laugh, because she was certain that he was talking about the maze, but it wasn't a bad idea for the entirety of their relationship, if she thought about it. They twisted and turned through the passageways, Rowan jumping every time a leaf brushed against her neck. Eventually, she saw sunlight up ahead and breathed a sigh of relief. She'd started to wonder if she was going to be sleeping in the maze tonight.

But when they reached the opening in the trees, she hesitated.

'Oh, right, I'd started to suspect as much…' Jonathan said behind her.

Because they weren't back at the entrance. They had found the centre of the maze. It was bathed in sunshine so bright that Rowan had to shield her eyes—which had grown used to the gloom—with her hand. She stepped out of the shade of the maze towards the love seat at the centre of the clearing. Climbing roses had been left to creep around the archway over it, and it was covered in enormous white, pink and yellow blooms.

She couldn't help herself. She walked

towards it and sat, swinging slightly back and forth, her long legs easily reaching the ground.

'You look like a painting.'

Jonathan's voice took her by surprise. She hadn't realised that he had followed her over, and she looked up. And she'd never heard him sound quite like that before either. His voice was still low, but it was softer now, intimate. The sun was behind him, casting him in silhouette, all tall and slim, his body long flowing lines and easy grace.

'Room for two?' he asked, and she shifted over without a word, not quite trusting herself to speak. They swung in silence for a while, enjoying the sunshine, Rowan turning her face up to soak in the warmth.

'Thank you,' Jonathan said at last, and Rowan turned to look at him.

'What for?'

'For helping. For understanding when I asked you not to tell Liv. For making me get out for a bit. I can't remember the last time I just sat and did nothing.'

She smiled back at him, a little cautiously, surprised that he was opening up to her. 'You're welcome. On all counts. I'm glad that I can help. It…hurt, to see you that way this morning. I only wish I could do more.'

She held her breath, not sure whether she had said too much, given away too much about how she still felt for him. But she had been hiding her feelings for so long, and hadn't got over him even a little. If she wanted things to change, she had to change the patterns of behaviour that she'd clung to all that time. If she wanted him to come to her, she was going to have to make herself vulnerable, at least just a little.

'I… Do you really think I should tell Liv? And Caleb?' Jonathan asked.

Rowan took a deep breath, aware of the trust that Jonathan was placing in her to ask this. How easily he might close off again if she misstepped.

'I suppose…' she started. 'I suppose I'm less focused on you actually telling her than on the fact that you feel that you can't. Liv is tough, you know. Resilient.'

'I know that,' Jonathan said, and Rowan couldn't mistake the feeling of pride she saw on his face when he spoke about his sister. 'It's not that I think she *couldn't* deal with it. It's that I don't want her to have to.'

Rowan nodded, understanding him a little better. But she couldn't agree with him. 'I'm sure that if she did know what was going on, she wouldn't want you to have to deal with it either, never mind dealing with it completely alone. She cares about you as much as you care about her.'

He huffed something that she thought was probably intended to be a laugh but came out as something much sadder.

'Oh, Jonathan.' She reached for his hand and squeezed, because she could see that he was hurting, and she couldn't help herself. 'I hope you know that she cares about you.'

'She hates me, Rowan. You don't have to sugar-coat it. Our relationship was never going to be the same after Mum and Dad left and I had to be responsible for them. I came to terms with it a long time ago.'

'But it doesn't have to stay that way,' she said gently. 'You're *not* responsible for them any more, or at least no more responsible for them than they are for you. Why don't you share the burden? Tell them what's going on and see if they can help. They can offer their support, even if there's nothing practical they can do.'

He didn't say no immediately, and she supposed she would have to leave it at that. She knew him well enough to know that he would need to mull it over. Jonathan had never been one for snap decisions.

They swung back and forth a couple more times, and Rowan looked up at the flowers above her head, marvelling at how nature had created something so beautiful left entirely to her own devices.

'I think it might be magic in here,' she said, not thinking before she spoke. 'It's so beautiful it doesn't feel real.'

'I think you're right,' Jonathan said, shifting round slightly to look at her. 'I think the whole world could disappear while we were in here and we wouldn't know. Or care.'

She allowed herself a small, hopeful smile, turning her face towards him.

'You know, I quite like the sound of that.'

He reached for her hair again, and she gritted her teeth. 'Another cobweb?' she asked, frozen in place.

'No. Just…you,' he replied, twisting the lock of hair around his finger. 'Is that okay?'

'Yeah,' Rowan breathed, afraid that anything else would break the spell of this fairytale place. Perhaps they could just stay, she thought.

And then Jonathan's hand slid more firmly into her hair and she stopped thinking at all.

He was going to kiss her. She had never been more certain of anything in her life. She had been here before, and he had no reason now to think that she didn't know what she was doing. He was taking his time about it, and she knew that he was thinking, overthinking. But she could be patient, give him the time that he needed to know that he wanted this.

His head dipped, his gaze fixed on her lips, and she held her breath.

But as he leaned in, her phone started to buzz, and she resisted the urge to groan out loud.

'Is that you?' Jonathan asked, an edge of frustration in his voice.

'My alarm,' she replied, real life breaking through the trees into their hideaway. 'For Liv's pain meds.'

'I'm sure that Caleb…' Jonathan started to suggest, but the spell had been broken and they both knew it.

'We should probably get back,' Rowan said, trying to hide how desperately disappointed she was.

'Right, yes, of course. I know the way out from here,' Jonathan said, in a distracted tone that betrayed how thoroughly the atmosphere between them had shattered.

She followed him back out and up to the house, watching his long legs in his slim-cut jeans while trying to see in her peripheral vision whether he was watching her too.

When they were alone, when they caught each other's eyes, something changed about the air, making it harder to pull it into her chest, so she could feel herself struggling to keep it even, to keep her body from arching towards his, following some deeply held impulse to be close to him.

'I should…' Jonathan said, moving towards the door.

'Yes. Of course. I'll see you later, I suppose.'

She was standing in front of the door, she realised, when Jonathan didn't leave the room. She took a step to her left as Jonathan moved in the same direction, and she found herself chest to chest with him. His hands came to her upper arms and she was sure he was going to move her to the side, but then didn't. Instead, his thumbs were skimming over the smooth skin along her arm, making her shiver and want to press closer to him, and she might have done so if it wasn't for the sound of shoes on the flagstones behind her.

She spun around at the same moment that Jonathan stepped back and dropped her arms, the flaming red of her face meaning that they weren't exactly the picture of innocence. Luckily, Caleb had his eyes on his phone and by the time he looked up they were decent.

'Liv's awake,' he said, grinning at them. 'I'm going to make sandwiches for lunch.'

'Great. Thanks,' Rowan said, finding it impossible to get her voice to its usual pitch. 'I'll check on her.'

They were all at the table, passing Caleb's impressive doorstop sandwiches around, Rowan desperately trying to avoid meeting Jonathan's eye and give away what had happened—what had almost happened—

in the maze when Liv gasped in shock and slapped her forehead with her hand.

'Oh, God, I've only just thought about your race!' Liv declared, startling them all. 'How the bloody hell am I going to do it on crutches? Caleb, do you think you could drive—?'

'I'm really sorry but I have a thing on Saturday. I can't back out now,' he said, around a mouthful of cheese and pickle.

'It's fine,' Rowan said, putting her hand over Liv's. 'There's a bag drop. I'll prep all my stuff before I leave and they'll make sure it's waiting for me at the aid stations.'

'But you need me there!' Liv insisted. 'To remind you to eat and to change the batteries in your torch and to put on fresh clothes when you're gross.'

Rowan laughed at her friend's assessment of their friendship. She wasn't far wrong. 'And I love having you on my team,' she told her truthfully, because Liv had been there at every one of her ultras, and she had no doubt that she wouldn't have finished them without her. 'But you're injured, so you're going to sit this one out. You would tell me just the same if things were the other way around. You know you would.'

'I'll do it,' Jonathan said. She whipped her head around and stared at him, realising as she did that Liv and Caleb were doing the same. He shifted a little uncomfortably under their combined scrutiny. 'You don't all need to look so surprised.'

'Jonathan,' Rowan said softly, trying not to give anything away with her voice. 'That's really generous but it's a long race. I'll be happy if I manage it in twenty-four hours. I can't ask that of you.'

'You didn't ask,' he said, his voice terse. There was no sign of the softness that she'd heard in the maze. 'I'm insisting. You need a support crew and I'm happy to do it. So, I'm not sure that there's anything more to talk about.'

She gaped at him. There was no way that she could let Jonathan do that for her. But he didn't seem to be listening.

'Anyway, I suspect that if I don't do it then Liv will insist on hobbling after you on crutches. This way I know that she's resting her ankle.'

Rowan stared at him, sure that if she

could make him blink that he would change his mind. But the longer she looked, the longer he looked back, until she felt heat rising in her cheeks. 'Jonathan, I... I...'

'Good. Thank you. Let's not talk about this any more, shall we?'

She opened her mouth to do just that, but Jonathan's hand landed on hers, and she was so shocked she couldn't speak.

'Did you find anything interesting in the boxes we brought through from the library?' Jonathan asked Liv, withdrawing his hand from Rowan's as he turned away.

Fortunately, Caleb was focused on his lunch, but her glance across at Liv confirmed that her friend had seen *something*, even if she didn't know what it was.

'I don't know,' Liv said. 'Maybe. Did you know that Great-grandmother was going to launch a perfume line before the war? I've found minutes from meetings that suggest they had formulations, bottles, packaging, everything ready to go. Then the paper trail just ends and I don't know what happened.'

'That sounds interesting,' Rowan said, jumping on the change of subject. 'And they didn't go back to it after the war was over?'

'Not as far as I can see. Jonathan, do you know anything about it?'

He shook his head. 'First I've heard of it. As far as I'm aware we've never branched out into fragrance or cosmetics.'

'Well, maybe we should,' Liv said, and then immediately blanched.

'Well, there's an idea,' Rowan said thoughtfully. 'Multibillion-pound industry. Decent margins. You've got an established prestige brand. There are far worse moves you could make.' Rowan glanced at Jonathan, wondering how he was taking this. She hadn't given away anything that he'd asked her not to, but she wasn't going to let an opportunity to help Jonathan talk to Liv pass without making the most of it.

'I've offered you a job before, Liv. You've never shown any interest in taking an active role in the family business. This sounds like it would require a lot of investment,' Jonathan observed in a carefully neutral voice. 'I'm not sure that now would be the time.'

Liv narrowed her eyes at him. 'Why? Is there a problem with the business?'

Jonathan shook his head and Rowan resisted the urge to sigh.

'It just sounds like a risk.'

'Well,' Rowan said, cutting in before Liv and Jonathan could return to their well-worn path of sniping at each other. 'It's an idea. Maybe you should both think it over. See if anything else turns up in those boxes. We can work through some more in the library this afternoon and we'll send stuff through to you if it looks like it might be relevant.'

When she walked through to the library with Jonathan after lunch, she wasn't sure what sort of reception to expect.

'That was promising,' she commented, picking up a pile of papers and sorting them, half an eye out for anything to do with perfumes or fragrance. But Jonathan stayed quiet for so long that she had to give in and look up at him.

'I don't disagree,' he said, his expression a little defensive.

'And is that the same as you agreeing?' Rowan asked, softening the remark with a smile.

'It would require a lot of investment.' Jonathan leaned back in his chair, his fingertips going to massage the orbits of his eye sockets in a way that felt endearingly familiar.

'You mentioned that already. But it could generate a lot of income as well. A whole new revenue stream. Surely it's worth investigating.'

'I just don't know when…or how…or…' He trailed off, his forehead creasing.

'So delegate it,' she suggested with a shrug, wondering whether she would have to explain the word to him.

'To Liv?'

'It's worth asking, surely?'

Jonathan shook his head. 'I can't see how I could do that without telling her about the problems with the business.'

'That's up to you. It's all up to you, of course. I just want you to see that you have the option there, if you want it. Liv is talented. She's freelanced product launches for a dozen companies. She's more than qualified.'

'That's not in doubt,' Jonathan replied dryly. Rowan came to stand beside him and resisted the urge to reach out and smooth the tension she could see pulling at his features. 'But there's no way in hell she would come and work for me. I've asked her before, when she left university. She said she didn't want me trying to control her at work as well as at home.' Rowan winced, remembering that particular episode. 'How have I messed things up so badly with her? I only ever wanted to protect her, and now we can barely have a civil conversation. I can't imagine any situation where she would want to work for me.'

Rowan's heart clenched, and this time she couldn't not reach out and put a hand on his shoulder. 'Liv doesn't hate you.' She would normally hesitate to speak for her friend. It wasn't her place to get in the middle of a family argument. But she couldn't leave Jonathan with the pain of believing that his sister hated him when Rowan knew it was so much more complicated than that, and probably not really about him at all.

'She doesn't,' she said again, squeezing his shoulder.

He huffed, and she wasn't sure if it was a laugh. 'She does a good impression of it.'

'I know. But it's not really you she's angry at.' Because she wasn't blind to her friend's faults, and she had been aware for a long time of how much animosity and anger was there. But she had enough objectivity to know that that didn't mean Liv hated him.

'She's always deserved so much better than I've been able to give her.'

'Jonathan,' Rowan said, her hand coming to cup his cheek this time, and tilting his face up so that he would look at her. 'All you've ever done, as far as I have seen, is try and take care of her.'

'And all that's done is drive her further and further away.'

Rowan gave him a grim smile, wishing she could do more. 'That's not your fault. I wish you could give yourself a break and see what I see.'

He smiled, and the shift of muscles under her palm reminded her of how close they had moved. Reminded her that she was supposed to be getting close. But she hadn't done this to be calculating. All she wanted was to ease the pain that she saw around his eyes. To comfort someone who was trying their hardest under difficult circumstances.

'You can't expect to find yourself at the head of a family and the head of a business when you're only in your twenties and get everything exactly right every time.'

Jonathan frowned. 'Ah, well, that's the thing, isn't it? Because when you have those responsibilities, getting it wrong isn't an option. The consequences are too dire. Mum and Dad left, and my grandparents were already in a care home and not in good enough health to take on their responsibilities. If I hadn't spent so much time looking after the business, then we would have lost everything. I couldn't have afforded Cal's school fees, or the care home fees, or Liv's student accommodation. They were already surviving the trauma of my parents leaving and I wasn't going to add to that with complete financial collapse or having to live with me full-time as well. I was so focused on saving the business that I didn't realise that I was getting things so wrong with Liv.'

'You did what you had to,' Rowan reminded him. 'You've been fighting on God knows how many fronts, trying to fix problems that you didn't cause. No one can blame you for not being perfect. Not even you. I won't allow it.'

Rowan couldn't believe that he had taken

all this on himself, when he had been the same age as she was now. She couldn't imagine what that sort of pressure did to a person.

'You were angry with me,' he reminded her, and she wasn't sure where that change of subject had come from. 'When I tried to stop you…making a mistake. With me.'

'You want to talk about that now?' she asked, raising an eyebrow, frustrated with him for changing the subject. 'I think we can do without rehashing my most embarrassing moments.'

'Embarrassing? What reason have you got to be embarrassed?' he asked. 'We never really talked about what happened, and now I'm thinking perhaps we should have done.'

'It's ancient history,' Rowan told him, not sure whether she wanted to hear his thoughts now that it came down to it.

'It wasn't that I didn't want—' he started, and she decided that maybe she would hear him out after all, because all these years she'd been haunted by the memory of him saying no, and if that hadn't come to him quite as easily as it had seemed to, then her ego could do with hearing it. 'You were so young,' he finished, and Rowan snorted.

'I was twenty-one. An adult,' she reminded him, in no uncertain terms. 'There's only seven years between us. Not that that stopped you calling me a kid.'

'I was trying to help! To point out that you'd get over it soon enough. Anyway, by the time I was twenty-eight I had parental responsibility for a girl the same age as you were then. I had responsibility for Cal—who was still at school, if you remember. That makes for a hell of a lot more difference than seven years does. Not to mention the fact that you'd been drinking. You weren't thinking straight.'

She racked her brains, trying to remember. Yes, they'd shared a bottle of wine, but she had been a student for three years and could drink a couple of glasses without her judgement being terminally affected. She'd known exactly what she was doing, and the fact that Jonathan thought she wasn't capable of judging that for herself—wasn't capable of *asking*, instead of assuming— was enraging. 'I'd had a couple of glasses of wine. I knew exactly what I was doing.'

'I know what you look like when you're tipsy. I spent enough time watching you that summer.'

Which was quite the admission, Rowan thought, watching how his cheeks pinked as he realised what he'd said.

She was twenty-one and had barely been kissed, never mind had someone fall in love with her. Unless she thought about those times where it felt like her and Jonathan were two sides of the same coin. When they laughed at the same obscure jokes, or caught one another's eyes across the room, and she felt that warm swell of intimacy between them.

So when she'd found them alone, enjoying one another's company, the evening feeling so *right*—she'd taken her chance to prove her bullies wrong. Only she hadn't. She'd shown herself that they had it right. If not even Jonathan—who she connected with on every other level—wanted to kiss her, then what hope did she have of ever finding someone who would think she was anything other than a freak?

'I couldn't kiss you when I didn't know if you were doing it because you really wanted to or because there was something else going on. I'm sorry. We really should have talked about this at the time.'

Jonathan was right. They should have talked about this before now.

'I should get back to work,' Jonathan said, pushing back his chair and standing up. 'If you... If you wanted to spend some more time in the library this afternoon—' he looked up and caught her eye '—I'd like that very much.'

CHAPTER SEVEN

IN THE END, she had spent most of the afternoon in the library, looking for any signs of the long-forgotten fragrances in the older papers, and any sign of how the company had got into its current financial difficulty in the present. The former she'd given to Liv, who had taken up residence in the family room, and the latter she'd pored over herself, talking with Jonathan in quiet tones so that they wouldn't be overheard. They'd eaten dinner in there too—Liv had fallen asleep while watching a movie and they hadn't wanted to disturb her, and Cal was up in his room.

The whole evening had such an air of intimacy, as they had worked, and eaten, and—when she could tease one from Jonathan—laughed together, that the prospect of sleeping in Jonathan's bed come nightfall felt a little more loaded than it had when they'd agreed to it that morning.

She hesitated outside of his bedroom door, aware of the sound of him moving round inside. It was one thing telling herself that morning that sleeping in Jonathan's bed wouldn't mean anything, but it was quite another to be standing on his threshold, listening to him in his room and building up the courage to knock. Especially after all they had been through today. Not least that moment in the maze when she had been sure that he was going to kiss her—which had been playing on a loop in the back of her mind, even as she worked through his accounts.

It was only the sound of footsteps moving towards her from inside the room that prompted her into action. The only thing worse than lifting her hand to knock at this point would be being discovered lurking here like some kind of blushing schoolgirl.

She knocked quickly, and Jonathan opened the door a fraction of a second later, and almost barrelled into her. She lifted her hands instinctively and found herself stumbling backwards until Jonathan's arm reached around her waist and stopped her falling.

'Rowan!' Jonathan exclaimed as they tried to find their balance, reclaim their hands and pretend that their bodies weren't touching from chest to knee. 'I'm sorry, I wasn't expecting you to be there,' he said, stating the obvious while refusing to make eye contact.

'You said I could sleep in here so I don't have to spend the night on the sofa,' she reminded him. 'If you've changed your mind, it's fine. I can—'

'Of course. I hadn't forgotten,' Jonathan said, taking a step backwards so he was firmly in the landing while she hovered in the doorway, not sure which direction she should be moving in. The movement had brought their bodies close together, and there was a hum of awareness all over her skin as she waited for him to move away. Was she brave enough to ask him to stay? Yesterday, she wouldn't have been. But yesterday felt like a different world. One where he hadn't told her that he was attracted to her, and that the only reason he had pushed her away that first time was to try and protect her. She looked up and met his eye just as he took a half step backwards, and she lost her nerve.

'Make yourself at home,' Jonathan said in a low gravelly voice, gesturing into the room. 'There are clean sheets on the bed, and there's extra firewood in the basket by the hearth if you want it. That door leads into the bathroom but remember to lock the door to the hallway.'

She didn't think that she could blush any harder than she already was—until, that was, she pictured herself in the huge copper free-standing bathtub, surrounded by bubbles and lit by endlessly flattering candles. Her eyes closed until she was startled by a sound in the doorway, and opened them to find Jonathan watching her, an interested look on his face.

'Rowan?' Real Jonathan said, sadly distracting her from the far more easily seduced fantasy version.

'Bathroom door,' she said, remembering the last thing that he had told her and hoping her thoughts weren't showing too obviously on her face. 'Got it.'

Then they ran out of conversation and were both just staring at each other. 'I'll, um.

I'll leave you to it,' Jonathan said awkwardly, trying to pretend that they weren't both standing there thinking about her climbing into his bed, sinking into his mattress. When he walked away, she stood at the door for a moment watching him retreat. Wondering what it would have taken to be closing the door on the world *together*. Locking themselves in with the fire and the sweet-smelling sheets and the drapes pulled across the curtains and around the bed. Creating a space for them to…be.

She'd let herself imagine scenes like that once. When she had first nurtured and nursed her crush on him. When she thought that the looks that they exchanged and jokes that they shared were building towards something. It would be easy to fall back into thinking like that, she acknowledged. To remember how easy things had felt between them once. But that only led her thoughts back to how he had rejected her, which was very much not where she wanted them to be just now.

She got ready for bed with resolute determination to pretend that everything was perfectly normal, and that sleeping in the bed of the person she'd been crushing on her whole adult life was completely unremarkable to her. It was only as she slid into the sheets and found herself engulfed by Jonathan's familiar scent that she realised how much trouble she was in. It shouldn't smell of him because the sheets were fresh, she told herself. Which did absolutely nothing to dampen the physical reaction she was having to finding herself in a veritable cloud of Jonathan. But imagined or not, it was going to make it impossible to convince herself that she was in anyone else's bed but his.

When sleep eventually took her, her unforgiving subconscious whisked her straight back to that copper bathtub, Jonathan watching her from the doorway, looking as if he were waiting for the nod to climb in there with her and grant her every wish. Her hands followed where his eyes roamed. Bold with her body in fantasy in a way she hadn't yet learned to be in reality, her palms slicked through the mounds of bubbles on her breasts, her mouth ticking up on a smile at the sight of what that did to Jonathan's expression as he stood in the doorway, watching, with a look of fierce possessiveness she'd pay all her worldly goods to see on him in real life.

Her hands sank into the hot water as they spread over her stomach, and she gave Jonathan a smile that she hoped he realised meant, *Get yourself over here and do this for me.* Dream Jonathan didn't need telling twice and was on his knees beside the tub before she could form another thought.

His hand threaded into the artfully undone bun at the back of her head, of the sort that only existed in dreams, tilting her face towards him while the other sank below the water to do things with her body she'd only attempted solo.

Jonathan was a quick study and had her breathless and in danger of splashing all of the water out of the tub in outrageously short order. Because of course he was as wordlessly competent at this as he was at everything else he set his mind to. It was just at the point that she grabbed him by the shirt and pulled him into the tub on top of her, causing a tidal wave of ceiling-destroying proportions, that she woke with a start, panting into the cold air, sweat cooling on her skin. A door had slammed somewhere in the house, and if she ever found out who had disturbed her dream at the crucial moment, she would slam *them* into a door.

She turned her face into the pillow, and would have screamed out her frustration, if she hadn't got a faceful of Jonathan's scent. Really, how did he do that? She was tempted to just finish the job herself. But making herself come in Jonathan's bed was probably taking his offer of hospitality a step too far. Not to mention the fact that DIY was a lot less appealing when a moment ago she'd had a skilled craftsman applying himself to the job.

Thinking that way wasn't going to get her back to sleep, she acknowledged after tossing and turning for another half an hour. She needed to get up, make herself a cup of soothing tea and find something extremely dull to read to bore herself to sleep. She remembered the bookshelf of pulpy thrillers in the family room as she set the kettle on the range to boil and then crossed the hall to go and choose one.

She flicked on the light in the family room and let out a scream as a body rose from the sofa in the middle of the room and bellowed.

'Jonathan!' she called out, as she realised who was there. He was wearing a cotton T-shirt and tight black boxers, cut high over long thighs. She pulled her own hoodie down lower over her sleep shorts, wishing she'd taken the time to pull on joggers as well. Though by the way Jonathan's gaze seemed to have fixed on her legs he didn't seem to mind.

'Rowan, what are you doing in here?' Jonathan said, asking the obvious question that at least one of them needed to.

'I couldn't sleep,' she said in a rush. 'There was… I had a dream.' She stopped herself, hoping Jonathan wouldn't guess that she had been dreaming about him. And then realised none of that explained why she was there.

'Did you want to talk about it?' he asked, sitting back down on the couch. She winced in sympathy, remembering how uncomfortable she had been the night before.

'I was looking for something to read,' she blurted out, stepping into the room and crossing to the bookshelf. 'I couldn't get back to sleep.'

'Me neither,' Jonathan said with a wry

grin, that she couldn't help but return. They were interrupted by the whistle of the kettle, making Rowan jump.

'I was making tea,' she said, stating the obvious, delaying the moment they would say goodnight.

'I wouldn't say no to a cup,' Jonathan said, standing again and stretching. 'Might help this torture device seem less offensive.'

'What are you doing down here anyway?' Rowan asked in a low voice as they walked through to the kitchen. She grabbed a tea towel and pulled the kettle off the hot plate and Jonathan rummaged in a cupboard for mugs and teabags. 'I thought that you were sharing with Caleb.'

'Chamomile?' he asked her, dropping a bag into a cup, and she smiled, embarrassingly pleased that he remembered her favourite.

'Ah, well…' Jonathan looked uncomfortable, and Rowan gave him a questioning look.

'What?'

'I didn't exactly check with Caleb that he didn't mind me sharing his room before I offered you mine. He was very much against the idea. And, well, the sofa was the only other option.'

'The sofa is a terrible option,' Rowan said, sighing. 'I would never have accepted your room if I'd known you would end up sleeping there. I'll swap with you. Or go back in with Liv,' she said, as Jonathan carried the tea to the table. She sat beside him on the bench, tucking one foot underneath her and propping her chin on her knee as she wrapped her hands around the steaming mug.

'No,' Jonathan objected. 'Don't disturb Liv. She needs to rest.'

'Then I'll take the sofa,' Rowan countered. 'I won't sleep knowing that I've kicked you out of your bed.'

'Absolutely not,' Jonathan declared. 'I offered you my room. What sort of person would I be if I changed my mind now, in the middle of the night?'

Rowan groaned, because really she was too tired and too frustrated to get into an argument with Stubborn Jonathan just now. 'You'd be a reasonable person making life easier for a very tired person. I know what that sofa's like, remember? You've already spent half the night on there. It's only fair that we swap. Why can't you just agree that it's fair and let it drop?'

'Because fairness has nothing to do with it,' he said, catching her eye and holding her there. 'I gave you my word.'

Rowan rolled her eyes, trying to shake off his intensity. 'And your word is law? You said I could have your room because you thought you would be in Caleb's room. It didn't work out. This doesn't have to be a big drama.'

But Jonathan's expression didn't budge and he shook his head as he crossed his arms. 'And whose fault is it that I didn't check it was okay with Cal first? If you've any doubts, I'm sure that he or Livia would be pleased to enlighten you.'

Rowan groaned, because they were back here again when all she wanted to do was get to sleep. 'New rule,' she declared. 'You don't talk to me about Liv. No more talking to her about you. We build a wall. It's the only way I'm going to survive this.'

A hint of a smile ticked up the corner of his mouth and she narrowed her eyes at him, convinced in that moment she'd missed something. 'What?' she asked, suspicious about his abrupt change in mood.

'You talk to Liv about me?'

Damn. Walked straight into that one.

'Liv talks to me about you,' she amended, her head resting on her crossed arms on the table. '*Complains* to me about you. One-way traffic.'

'So you never told her about our...' She looked up, interested, as he trailed off, and wondered if he planned on finishing his sentence.

'I didn't think there was anything to tell,' she said carefully. Perhaps if he hadn't made it so clear that nothing like it was ever going to happen again, she would have felt like there was something to say. And since they'd been here? Nothing had happened, and Liv wouldn't thank her for sharing the things she'd been imagining might happen. If anything ever did...well, she'd worry about it then.

'No. Well,' Jonathan said, his cheeks a little pink, and she realised that she liked him a little bit embarrassed. When he lost his air of certainty and let her see the human being underneath.

'I really need to get some sleep,' she said, letting her head rest back on her arms and wondering if it would be so bad to sleep here at the table.

'Of course. You go up, I'll turn the lights out in a minute,' Jonathan said, taking their mugs over to the sink.

'I thought I was taking the sofa,' Rowan murmured into her forearm.

'I thought I had made it clear that I had no intention of letting a guest in my home sleep on a sofa. It's bad enough that you slept there last night.'

Rowan pushed herself upright and gave him the sternest look she could manage while being really quite bleary-eyed. 'I'm perfectly capable of deciding for myself where I'm happy to sleep.'

Jonathan rested his hands on the table and leaned in. 'You're spending the rest of the night in my bed if I have to carry you there myself. Now would you please stop arguing and let me take care of you?'

Rowan let her mouth fall open and stared at him, shocked by the strength of feeling in his outburst. And then her brain helpfully hijacked her with a slideshow of Jonathan sweeping her up in his arms and carrying her up to bed and taking care of her in a variety of different ways. She was too shocked to even say anything, and stood looking at him, waiting for the penny to drop.

'Rowan, I'm sorry,' he said, starting to look awkward. 'I didn't mean to imply...'

'No, it's fine,' she said, reaching out to him, an idea occurring to her. 'You know, the bed is plenty big enough for the both of us, just for one night. Only half a night now. We can sort something else for tomorrow.' And, well, if she wanted him to kiss her again, there were worse ways to make that happen than to share a bed and see if it led anywhere.

'I don't know...' he said, the conflict on his face easy enough to read. He didn't want to spend the rest of the night on the sofa any more than she did, but he didn't want to overstep either.

'We don't need to make a big thing of it,' she said, not wanting him to get the wrong idea. 'I was sharing with Liv before and none of us thought anything of that.' Because there was no way that she was going to make a move on him—plan or no plan. If she was suggesting sharing his bed, she was also going to wait for him to make the first move.

He gave her a fierce, heated look that told her this was different, and she was perfectly aware why.

'I don't want to take advantage,' he said gruffly.

'You're not. I'm insisting,' she told him, holding out a hand for him to pull her up from the bench.

'If you insist, then I suppose I don't have a choice,' he said, taking her hand and pulling until she was standing in front of him. So close they were almost touching. They were being so careful with one another, and she didn't know how to stop.

Rowan had never felt more aware of her body than she did in those moments when she was climbing the stairs with Jonathan behind her, knowing that they were about to go to bed together. Jonathan hadn't stopped by the library to pick up any more clothes, and she realised she was happier being the one with legs on show, instead of having to try and keep her eyes off Jonathan's back-side in those boxers. At least under his heavy duvet, he would be safely out of view and she wouldn't have to rely on her self-control. But then again, she wasn't sure that being tucked under the covers with Jonathan was going to be enormously helpful when it came to making good decisions. 'Are you sure about this?' Jonathan asked by the door to his bedroom, so seriously that you could have believed she had suggested an amateur appendectomy, rather than two old friends sharing a bed for a few hours. She reached past him to open the door.

'Come on. It's late. I want to get *some* sleep tonight.'

She slid under the duvet and pulled off her hoodie, turning her back and trying not to imagine what Jonathan looked like as he slid into bed behind her. She allowed herself to imagine his arm coming around her waist, pulling her against him, her back to his chest, their bodies matched inch for inch right down to their ankles. Eventually, she felt him climb in beside her, felt the dip of the mattress and held her breath, wondering if either of them was going to break this stalemate. But soon she heard his breaths slow into the gentle, rhythmic sound of sleep, and she closed her eyes tight and tried every trick she knew to make oblivion come.

CHAPTER EIGHT

WHEN JONATHAN WOKE the next morning, it was to armfuls of Rowan. Her chest against his and the smooth skin of her legs tangled with his own. He should move away from her. He had known even as he had climbed into bed with her last night that this was a hopeless idea. He'd known that his self-control wouldn't be able to hold with her this close. He still remembered all the reasons why this was a bad idea. Why letting himself fall for Rowan could never work. He couldn't take care of his family and keep the business afloat *and* be a good partner to someone else. He already had more responsibilities than he could handle, and the very last thing he should be thinking about was adding more to his life.

But at the same time, he couldn't make any of that matter.

He still hadn't been able to gather the

strength to do what he knew he had to when her eyes blinked open, millimetres from his. They widened, startled, as she realised where she was, and he tightened his arms around her waist instinctively.

'You're in my bed,' he whispered, stating the painfully obvious. He expected her to jump from him as soon as she realised how close they had moved in the night. One of Rowan's thighs was already trapped between his legs, and he couldn't think of a single thing on earth that would make him want to move away. By some apparent miracle, it seemed Rowan must feel the same. Because instead of scrabbling away from him as he feared she would do after he'd pointed out where they both found themselves, she gave a contented sigh and lay warm and relaxed in his arms, her nose practically brushing against his.

Her tongue darted out to wet her lower lip. She was so close that he could only just see it in his peripheral vision. He closed his eyes, tightened his arms around her waist again and refused to think of all the reasons he shouldn't be doing this as he closed the distance between them and brushed his lips against hers. He sighed into the kiss as Rowan's hands crept up to his shoulders, her legs tangling even more tightly with his own.

As she moved against him, he became aware of just how long he had been waiting to do this. How long he had been denying himself even the knowledge of what he wanted. For the longest time, Rowan's infrequent and unannounced visits to the home that he had shared with Livia and Caleb during the holidays had been the highlight of a period of his life that had been characterised by unlooked-for responsibilities and unparalleled stress.

He'd realised too late after he'd rejected her without properly explaining himself and the reasons he couldn't allow himself the luxury of falling in love with her—because he couldn't imagine indulging this need for her leading anywhere else. He loosened an arm from around her waist and felt a shiver of possessiveness and desire at her groaned dissent, which was only quelled when he tangled his fingers into her hair and angled her mouth so that he could plunder it more thoroughly.

It was just as he was wondering how efficiently he could get them both naked, desperate to have her closer, that the door to his bedroom swung open, and he and Rowan sprang apart, like magnets repelling one another.

'Rowan, could you give me a hand with—? Bloody hell!' Liv cried from the doorway, slamming her hands over her eyes and turning away. 'Sorry, I didn't realise... When you said you were sleeping in here, Row... Never mind, I'm going, I'm gone, I didn't see anything.'

Rowan jumped from the bed, revealing acres of leg that he really should have averted his eyes from. But that ship had well and truly sailed. 'Liv, hold up, it's not what you think,' Rowan said as she reached her friend, where Liv was struggling down the hallway on her crutches.

He wanted to call out to Rowan to come back. To leave Liv and get back in his bed where she belonged. But he couldn't ask that of her, not in front of his sister, at least. So he threw himself back on the pillow as Rowan talked to Liv in a low voice so he couldn't make out what she was saying. With an arm across his face for good measure, he tried in vain to remember why he had spent the past seven years trying not to think about kissing Rowan and could come up with nothing.

Rowan lingered over her shower, letting the hot water obliterate her senses, trying not to think about how it had felt that morning waking up with Jonathan and failing miserably. She tried focusing on the simplicity of sensation, the hot water on her skin, the steam she was breathing in. But all she could feel were Jonathan's hands on her sides and in her hair. Jonathan's mouth on hers and his breath in her lungs. It was only when the hot water tank gave out that she decided it would be childish to risk hypothermia by staying in the shower just because she was afraid of seeing the man she'd been kissing not an hour ago. It wasn't as if she regularly went round kissing people and then having breakfast with them as if nothing had happened.

This was what she had wanted to happen. A kiss that didn't end with him rejecting her, and then…the rest of her life. Without him in it.

When Liv had appeared in the doorway, expecting to find Rowan alone and looking for help with taking a shower, Rowan had let herself follow her instinct to chase after her and try and explain, and ignore the tug in her chest that was telling her to go back to Jonathan and pick up where they left off.

Liv had taken it well, all things considered. Rowan had told her what she knew, which wasn't much. That she and Jonathan had shared a bed because Caleb had kicked Jonathan out, and that the kiss wasn't planned and she didn't expect it to happen again.

Did she *want* it to happen again? Every part of her body was screaming yes, of course. She'd wanted this to happen pretty much since she'd arrived at the manor. She knew that Jonathan wouldn't hurt her on purpose. He knew now how much he'd hurt her the first time, and she didn't think he would be deliberately careless with her feelings. She had to keep reminding herself that all she wanted was a kiss that didn't end up with her heart being stamped on. A chance to move on with her life and get over him. And she'd had that. But they had a few more days in this house. A few more days when she could—if she had the courage—let herself feel desirable. Desired.

But she would have to be careful, she thought as she towelled herself dry. She'd been careless with her feelings around Jonathan once before, and she wouldn't make the same mistake again. She needed to get out for a run. Even if it was just a couple of miles to clear her head.

Fifteen minutes later she was pounding along one of the woodland paths, striving with every pace to find the flow that usually came to her so easily. But every metre felt like a struggle in a way she didn't recognise.

She consciously took stock of her body, trying to pinpoint the source of the problem. Her shoulders were tense and her fingers rigid, so she took a deep breath, trying to let go of the tension in her upper body, making herself more efficient. She concentrated on her affirmation, which always helped to quieten her thoughts and allow her first to exist in the moment. But today its magic seemed to have worn thin. Because the moments it most wanted to live in were the ones from early that morning, when she had been in Jonathan's bed, with the man she'd fantasised about for so long kissing her hard and exploring beneath her clothes before they'd been so abruptly interrupted. Instead of achieving zen and flow, her brain wanted her to consider all the possible places that kiss could have gone if they hadn't been disturbed, and whether she was ever going to get a chance to find out.

She'd chased after Liv so quickly that she'd not had a chance to see how Jonathan was feeling about what they'd done. Whether he regretted it. Again. She'd been so focused ever since on not letting him have a chance to reject her that she hadn't stopped to look and see how he was feeling about what had happened. She tried to concentrate on her stride but she was so in her head that she stumbled over a tree root and had to break her fall with her hands before she went face first into a patch of nettles.

She scrambled out of the stingers, her legs burning, wishing she'd worn her full-length tights, and sat at the foot of the tree, rubbing at her burning skin with a dock leaf.

It could be worse, she told herself, as a fiery rash bloomed and she squeezed her eyes shut to stop the tears. A broken ankle like Livia's would have had her out of training for more than a month. Her only real injury was to her pride. She mashed another dock leaf in her palm and rubbed it on her leg, her teeth cutting deep into her lip as she winced with every stroke over her skin. She pushed herself up from the ground and forced herself to jog back to the manor, knowing that she had to wash the sting off before it would get better. Even stopping for every good patch of dock leaves she saw wasn't going to be enough to calm her angry, inflamed skin.

By the time she reached the back door of the manor, her legs were bright red, streaked with green and covered in welts. Her hands were still stinging and stained green from dock leaves and her face was streaked from the tears she'd given up fighting back for the last half mile. She needed a cool flannel and a vat of lotion and somewhere dark and quiet to nurse her wounds.

'Oh, my God, what happened to you?'

Rowan barely stopped herself from falling and bashing her head on the flagstone floor at the sound of Jonathan's voice. Because of course today would be the day he took actual breaks from the library to do frivolous things like visit the kitchen and hydrate.

'It's not as bad as it looks,' she said, turning away from him to try and hide the worst of it because she knew full well that she looked a fright and she wasn't sure that she could cope with him seeing her like this on top of all the other knocks she had just endured. But Jonathan wasn't letting her get away with that. He took her by the shoulders and steered her into a chair and pulled her feet up onto the bench. 'Nettles?' he asked, running a gentle finger down the front of her shin, making her shiver and wince at once.

'Yes,' she gasped, fighting the urge to scratch at the burning sensation that followed.

'Wait here,' he instructed, and Rowan found that she didn't have the strength to argue. She dropped her face into her hands and scrubbed at the tear tracks on her cheeks.

'Are your legs the worst of it?' he asked, returning with a bowl of water and a cloth.

'And my hands,' Rowan said with a little sniff, holding them out for him to inspect.

'You poor thing,' he said, pressing a kiss

to first one muddy palm and then the other, leaving Rowan stunned into speechlessness. She hadn't known what to expect from him today: whether he would be cool and distant, whether he would push her away as firmly as he had the first time that they had kissed. Never in her wildest imaginations had she envisaged this, Jonathan being soft with her. And so tender. She watched as he dipped the cloth into the water and wiped at her grazed, blistered skin, and let out a groan of satisfaction as the cool water soothed the burning.

'Better?' he asked, inspecting her palm intently as he cleaned each graze, only looking up once it was done.

'Much,' she croaked, not trusting herself to say more than that. He left her hand in the bowl of cool water as he methodically worked on the other, and if it hadn't been for the trail of fire ants that felt like they were crawling up her shins, she could have lost herself in the pleasure of it.

'What's wrong?' he asked, his face tilting up with concern when she shifted her legs uncomfortably.

'I think my hands are okay now,' she said.

'Your shins?' Jonathan asked, reading her

mind. She bit down hard on her lip and nodded, resisting the urge to claw at her skin.

The first swipe of the cool cloth, from her knee down to her ankle, was a crashing wave of relief so strong that it brought a tear to her eyes. Jonathan followed that up with another cool slide of the cloth on her other leg, and she let her head fall back against the chair and her eyes shut as he took care of her.

'I didn't know that the countryside was so dangerous,' he observed, drawing a laugh from her, even though she kept her eyes shut. 'You and Liv are making it an art form.'

She hissed as he cleaned a graze on her knee, and she smiled as he mumbled some comforting nonsense as he did the other.

'I should know better than to run unfamiliar trails when I'm distracted,' she said as he worked. He looked up at her words, her admission.

'Why were you distracted?' he asked, all innocence, and she let out a breathy laugh. As if he didn't know. 'Do you want to talk about what happened?' he asked.

'Do *you* want to talk about it?' she shot back. After all, he was the one who had had plenty to say after the first time that they had kissed. Very strong opinions.

She should be breaking this off now. Wasn't that what she had wanted? Had planned? This was meant to have been a second chance at a kiss. A chance to leave things on her own terms this time so that she could stop asking herself 'what if' and finally move on. But…being interrupted hadn't been a part of her plan. To have it end like that, with her chasing Liv down the hallway trying to explain what she'd just seen. That wasn't the ending that she deserved, after all this time. She'd come into this looking for closure, and instead now all she had were more questions.

'I wouldn't say that talking is top of my to-do list,' she answered at last, catching Jonathan's eye and trying to look suggestive. She couldn't tell from his expression whether she had hit her mark. He was holding something back, that much was clear. But whether he was resisting telling her that he wanted her or he was going to knock her back again, she couldn't be sure. A sensible woman would bolt before he had a chance to reject her again. There was no way that a sensible woman would risk being rejected again. But he was kneeling at her feet, with her hands in his, and she didn't know how to make herself not want more of that.

'I think I want to hear that list,' he replied with a small smile. Small enough that it told her that he was fighting something bigger. But he was letting her have this, now, and she was going to take whatever was on offer.

'Hey, Rowan,' she heard Liv shout from the family room. 'Is that you? Can you come in here?'

When Liv had called her away, she'd assumed it was something to do with her broken ankle. She doubted she would have let anything other than a broken bone tear her away from Jonathan at that moment. But it turned out all she wanted was to ask whether Rowan wanted to watch a movie when she and Jonathan were finished in the library.

Sitting at one end of the back-breaking sofa later that night, with Jonathan mirroring her body language next to her, she was certain that saying yes had been a terrible idea. She had assumed that Jonathan would carry on working in the library, but to her and everyone else's surprise, he had shut his laptop not long after seven and come to find them all in the family room.

Did this mean that he thought last night had been the start of something, rather than the end? She'd spent all day hoping that it was, even if it was a something that would only last a few days. All she knew was that she wanted more of the kisses that they had shared that morning. More of the way that she had felt when she was in his bed and in his arms. The only thing was, she wasn't entirely sure how to get there from here, trying to sneak sideways glances at Jonathan from her side of the sofa.

She scratched absently at her shin, the nettle rash starting to bother her again. Until she found her fingers gently pulled away and trapped in Jonathan's palm, and looked up at him in surprise. 'It'll make it worse,' he said in a low voice so that the others didn't hear. 'Do you want me to fetch you something for it?' he asked, and she wanted to melt under his kindness.

'It's fine,' she whispered, not pulling away. Maybe this was how they got there, she thought to herself. With tiny moves towards each other in the dark.

Jonathan didn't move away either, other than to give her hand a quick squeeze back. And so they sat holding hands, Rowan feeling positively adolescent—if her adolescence had involved such things as holding hands with boys, rather than trying to make herself as small and unnoticeable as possible in the hope of avoiding her bullies. Or, at least, not offering them further ammunition.

When she started to scratch at her other leg, Jonathan drew her closer, his arm around her shoulders this time, and he ran his palm slowly up her shin. Sensation enough to distract her from the stings. She held her breath, not sure that she could take this intimacy from him when both of his siblings were in the room.

'Right,' Liv said, as soon as the movie finished. 'I'm going to bed.'

'Do you need me to hel—?' Jonathan started to offer, half rising from his seat before he was interrupted.

'No, I've got it,' Caleb said, jumping up and passing Liv her crutches, before helping her out of her chair. 'I think I'll turn in as well,' he said to no one in particular, even though it was barely past ten o'clock.

Jonathan watched them leave before he turned to her. 'So, Caleb knows too?' he asked with a resigned sigh.

'Liv must had told him something,' Rowan said, shrugging as she watched Liv reach the top step and hop out of sight.

'I didn't realise we were so newsworthy,' Jonathan observed dryly, turning to look at her.

Rowan felt her cheeks warm under his attention. 'Newsworthy is a bit strong,' she said with a smile. 'Nothing really happened. It was just a kiss,' she added, not sure whether she wanted him to agree with that sentiment or not.

It would have been more straightforward, she supposed, to simply ask him what he thought about the kiss that they had shared. But she couldn't quite bear risking his answer feeling like another rejection. 'I wouldn't call it nothing,' Jonathan contradicted her, taking her hand and using it to bring her closer, which lit a warm glow deep in her belly and gave her the confidence to ask her next question.

'What *would* you call it?' she asked.

'Well,' Jonathan said, once she was pulled back against his side. 'I suppose in simplest terms we *could* call it just a kiss,' he observed, picking up her hand, examining the palm, pressing a kiss there and then dropping their linked hands into his lap.

'And in more complicated terms?' she ventured, feeling brave.

'Then I suppose it's something that we started, and that I've been thinking about all day.'

'Thinking about…finishing?' she asked, the double meaning very much intended. She'd been thinking about it all day too, not even her nettle stings distracting her from her daydreams. Jonathan coughed in surprise and Rowan chuckled gently. She had always loved throwing him off guard, and this time was no exception.

'You don't want to know the things I've been imagining.'

Oh, now, that was where he was wrong. She wanted to know every single thing that he had imagined, and then make them come true. Until he decided to share, though, she had her own fantasies to work with. Taking a deep breath, she decided now was the time to start, and climbed into Jonathan's lap, her knees straddling his thighs, her hands coming to rest on top of his when they came naturally to her hips, leaving things entirely in her court when it came to what happened next.

She flushed with the knowledge of that power and shifted forward, threading her fingers into his hair and taking her time, watching his face as she shifted her hips to get comfortable, using her hands to tilt Jonathan's face, deciding on what she wanted first and the best way for her to take it. And all through it, Jonathan's hands were still on her hips, holding her close but not directing her movement, as if he was as intrigued by her suddenly taking control as she was.

She rubbed a thumb across his lips and followed the touch with her lips, so fleeting that it was gone before she had a chance to take in Jonathan's gasp, and the quick grasp of his hands on her hips.

'Taking your time?' he asked, his voice strained.

'We have all night,' Rowan replied, hoping very much that they did. Jonathan's hands dropped from her hips to the curve of her backside, gently tipping her towards him. An invitation, not an instruction. It was too tempting an invitation to ignore, and so she leaned in and kissed him again, more slowly this time, letting herself revel in the unhurried glide of her lips over his. The hint of salt from the popcorn they had shared, the red wine that he had been sipping throughout the night.

His arms wrapped tight around her waist, a double brace of hard muscle across her back, pinning her to his front and taking her weight, leaving her free to explore, to play and to test his resolve. He opened his mouth beneath hers, and she sought out his tongue with her own, and groaned when he licked into her mouth, her resolve to take control faltering when her entire body seemed to dissolve into jelly.

But Jonathan was there, right when she needed him, his hands on both sides of her face, angling her so that he could kiss her deeper and harder, until her hips were rocking against him of their own accord, and she was pulling at the hem of his T-shirt, desperate to get at what was underneath. When

Jonathan broke suddenly away, she looked down at him in shock, her breath coming quickly and her hair around her shoulders, her clothes creased where they had been caught in the tight press of their bodies.

She might have been embarrassed if it wasn't for the sight of Jonathan looking thoroughly debauched below her. His cheeks were flushed and his hair messy where she had run her hands through it. And his lips were red and swollen—she couldn't be sure why that made her want to bite them, only that it absolutely did.

'Are you okay?' he asked, and she had to laugh because she felt better than she had in her entire life. Not that she planned on being quite that effusive with her praise.

'I'm good,' she said simply. 'Are you?' she asked as well, it suddenly dawning on her that he had been the one who had put the brakes on. Doubt flooded through her in an instant and she glanced towards the door, wondering if there was a way to make a quick yet elegant exit from a man's lap, and if the technique still worked if one had the legs of a newborn foal.

Her face must have fallen, because Jonathan was suddenly alert, lifting her off him and putting her down on the sofa beside him. 'Are you okay?' he asked again, brushing hair back from her face and looking at her with genuine concern.

'I'm fine,' she said quickly. 'But if you don't want to… You stopped us,' she pointed out, waiting for the blow of his rejection.

'Oh, Rowan,' Jonathan said with a pained groan. 'I didn't do that because I wanted to stop. I just…' He glanced around him at the family room. 'I need to be sure that this is what you want. I don't know what I have to offer you. I don't know what we can make of this. I like you so much, Rowan, and I would never hurt you on purpose, but I have so much—'

'Shh,' Rowan said gently, her fingers finding his bottom lip. 'It doesn't have to be anything you don't want it to be. I'm not thinking past this minute,' she told him.

He stared up at her for several long seconds, and for a moment she thought that he was going to change his mind. But then his hands found her hair again, and he was murmuring in her ear as he dropped kisses along her jaw. 'Then let's take this somewhere with a lock on the door. I don't really want to be interrupted again.'

'Oh.' Rowan sighed, realising probably far later than she should have that both Liv and Caleb had gone to their respective rooms with no mention of sharing with either of them. It seemed that everyone else in the family was expecting her to share Jonathan's bed that night, even if they themselves hadn't talked about it. 'I'm still not entirely convinced that this is really happening.'

The corners of his mouth turned up and he pulled her into a gentle kiss, one hand warm and comforting against her cheek.

'Definitely feels real,' he said, kissing her a second time, and then a third.

'You were thinking of moving this upstairs,' she reminded him, as his other hand slid under her and lifted her up and across, so that she was on top of him again.

'I have the best ideas,' Jonathan said, standing suddenly, so that she had to clutch at him with her arms around his neck and her legs locked around his waist as he carried her up the stairs, into his room, and kicked the door closed behind him.

CHAPTER NINE

SHE KEPT HER arms tight round his neck as he lowered her gently onto his bed, and the smell and feel of the sheets summoned memories of waking up wrapped around him that morning.

His long legs had been wrapped around hers, and she wanted to feel her skin on his like that again.

She tried to get a hand between them to make that happen, but he was too close, and so she contented herself with running a hand up his back under his T-shirt, pulling at the waistband of his jeans so that he could be in no doubt about what she wanted and how. He broke away, panting, and before she could lose her nerve, she threw off her T-shirt and pulled him back down, hiding her body from him before she had a chance to be self-conscious.

She reached for the hem of his shirt too, wanting to level the playing field. Because she couldn't be embarrassed about her state of undress if she got him naked too. The next minutes were a blur of kisses broken only by clothes being pulled off and sharp intakes of breath and long, muffled groans. Of doing battle with stubborn buttons and zips, until somehow, she was breathless and desperate for him, and Jonathan was above her, his weight on his elbows as he ravished her with kiss after kiss after kiss.

'Jonathan,' Rowan said, her hand on his chest holding him back, just for a moment as he scrabbled in his bedside drawer for a condom.

'What is it?' he asked, dropping his forehead to rest against hers. 'Do you want to stop?'

'No, God, no,' Rowan said, which produced a satisfied grin from Jonathan. 'It's just…' She hesitated, because this was putting it all on the line. She didn't have to tell him, but she wanted to. Wanted him to know what this was for her.

'I haven't done this before,' she said in a rush, before she could change her mind.

Jonathan stilled instantly and she groaned, thinking that he was about to pull away. Her hands found the small of his back and held him close.

This was her first time? For a second, the pressure of knowing that was overwhelming, before he realised that it didn't change anything, not really. He wanted her first time to be perfect for her. But he'd want that for her second and third and every time after that. She deserved nothing less. And if she was sure that she wanted this, then who was he to second-guess that.

He rested his forehead against hers a moment longer, and she watched him bite his bottom lip before he spoke.

'You want to?' he asked. 'You're sure?'

'I'm so sure,' she said in a rush, reaching up to kiss him, a hand cupping the back of his neck. 'I want to. I want *you*. Please?'

Her words hit him straight in the chest. Because they were so close to the rhythm that his heart was pounding out. He wanted her. He needed her. He had not a single doubt about this, despite every reason he knew that he should be thinking better of this.

He groaned. 'If you're going to ask so nicely...'

He took his weight on his elbows, moving his face back so that she could see every line of concentration around his eyes, the tick of a muscle in his jaw as he held himself so tightly in check. She moved her hand from his nape to his jaw, stroking the muscle there.

'Hey,' she murmured in a low voice. 'It's okay, I'm not going to break.'

She followed her thumb with her lips, kissing along his jaw until she reached his mouth.

'I don't want to hurt you.'

'I know. And you won't,' she said on a breath. 'You can trust me. Trust yourself.'

Jonathan made a noise that was somewhere between a groan and a laugh as he buried his face in her neck. Her skin tasted so good. He wanted to kiss every inch of it, but he wasn't going to rush this. Wasn't going to waste this chance to know her, in case it was the last one that he had. He took his time getting to know her body, what made her gasp, what made her moan, what made her grab his shoulders and urge him on.

When there was no part of her that he hadn't kissed or touched, whispered to or stifled a groan on. When she had begged, and asked nicely, and then given a growl of frustration and taken things into her own hands, he sank so slowly inside her that she had to clutch at his shoulders and pull him into a deep kiss.

She gasped aloud at the unfamiliar sensations, and bracketed Jonathan's face with her palms, kissing and kissing with a desperate urgency she hadn't realised she was capable of. When Jonathan broke their kiss, it was only to brush her hair back from her face and stare at her, as if she was something rare and precious. And he had never before wanted anything this much.

It was so much more intense than he had ever allowed himself to imagine. He suspected that he had always known that it would be like this. That they moved together, spoke to one another, *knew* each other in a way that he hadn't known existed, before tonight. That being with her felt like every broken part of him had found where it fit with a part of her. That together they were so much more than two stupid people who had stumbled around one another for too long. And he knew, with a certainty that terrified him, that he would never have this with another person. That whatever it was he had discovered here with Rowan tonight was unique to them.

Afterwards, when she lay in his arms, her skin damp and cooling, her limbs soft and spent, he refused to let himself think about what came next. Because in this moment of calm and quiet, she was perfect, and so was he.

CHAPTER TEN

JONATHAN WAS STILL sleeping when Rowan woke the next morning, and she permitted herself the indulgence of watching him for a few minutes. Last night had been everything that she had dreamed and hoped that it would be. It had been perfect, and the shadow of that hung over her now. Because where did one go from perfect? The only possible direction was down, and she wasn't sure that she had the heart to let anything taint her memories of the night before. She wanted to preserve it complete and unspoiled. If she let this play out without taking control now, she was going to get hurt. She was suddenly struck with the certainty of it, and the certainty of how devastating it would be for this to go wrong.

She rested her head against Jonathan's chest, a consolation prize for what she knew she would have to do next. She was going to have to get up, out of this bed, and tell him that this couldn't happen again. It would take every ounce of her resolve to drag herself into the shower and wash his scent off her skin, and the fact that she was even thinking that should have been enough to prove to her that she was making the right decision. Because how much worse would it be to walk away after two nights like this one? Three? She wouldn't want to do it, which would mean that Jonathan would have to be the one to end things. To reject her. And she wasn't sure that she could do that to herself again. No.

Right now, the most important thing was to remember what her priorities were: fixing the holes in her self-esteem that had resulted from Jonathan walking away from their kiss all these years ago. Getting over him. Moving on.

Well. Job done. Very well and thoroughly done, as it happened. She slipped from the bed and pulled on some clothes, and then headed straight for the bathroom before she could talk herself out of it.

Jonathan's door was still shut when she

was showered and dressed and she headed down the stairs and into the kitchen for breakfast, not allowing herself to think about whether she wanted him to be in there or not. Of course she wanted him, but what she didn't want, couldn't bear, was the thought of being rejected by him. She had to quit before she got hurt, however much she might be tempted to wish for more.

'Hey,' Jonathan said as she walked into the kitchen, and she squealed, jumping out of her skin. She hadn't heard anyone moving about the house, and had just assumed that Jonathan was still in bed where she'd left him.

'Hey,' Rowan replied quietly, feeling surprisingly tongue-tied. 'I didn't realise you were up.'

'I woke and you weren't there.'

Rowan shifted a little uncomfortably under his intense gaze. 'It was early. I didn't want to disturb you,' she lied, hoping that he would take her excuse at face value.

'Right,' Jonathan replied, his inflection free from emotion. He moved closer, and for a moment she thought that he was going to kiss her, but something must have made him change his mind, because he took a step away from her.

'So…you're okay, then?' he asked. 'After last night?'

'Of course,' Rowan admitted. 'I'm fine. Are you?'

He stared at her, and she would have given anything for him to smile at her just then.

'So you didn't leave because something was wrong?' he asked. 'I didn't… I wasn't…'

'You were perfect,' she said, suddenly realising how he had interpreted her early departure that morning. She couldn't leave him thinking that, but she also knew what she had to do.

She took a deep breath and forced out what she needed to say. 'It was fun, Jonathan, and really, really…' She searched for the right word, but knew that she couldn't do justice to what it had meant to her without giving away too much about what she felt for him. 'It was lovely. I'm glad that we're friends, but I think anything more than that would be too complicated, what with Liv and family stuff… You know?'

'Oh.' Jonathan's face fell, and for a moment she wondered whether she had actually hurt him. Before she remembered that this hadn't meant the same thing to him as it did to her. It was surprise, and nothing more, that had put that expression on his face. 'Yes. Right. You're probably right,' Jonathan said, rubbing at the back of his neck with an expression that made her wonder if they should have talked about expectations before they slept together, rather than waiting for the morning after.

But that was absurd. Even the idea that she could hurt Jonathan was ridiculous. He frowned at her, and asked again, 'And you're sure that last night was…okay?'

'It was perfect, Jonathan, honestly. I just don't think we need to make a big deal out of this.' She made herself turn her mouth up in a smile, even though it was the last thing that she felt like doing.

'I just need… I need to move on,' she said at last.

It was perfect.

Jonathan replayed the words over and over in his head as Rowan took her plate of toast and her coffee and went off to find Liv. He sat back at the table and reran the whole night in his head. It had been…dreamlike. Or it had been for him, at least. He had thought that Rowan had enjoyed it every bit as much as he had but… Well, he must have done something wrong, or she wouldn't have snuck out at dawn and then made clear at the earliest opportunity that she never wanted it to happen again. He felt an uncomfortable pang of conscience.

He shouldn't have just rushed in yesterday without thinking through the consequences. Without weighing up what he and Rowan meant to one another. Without talking carefully about what this meant for Rowan's friendship with Liv, never mind his own relationship with his sister. Because, despite her assurances that everything was fine, there was no hiding from the fact that Rowan had been strange and awkward with him, and he had the distinct feeling that he had hurt her without knowing how.

He got to work in the library and looked up in surprise when he heard Rowan clear her throat behind him later that afternoon. She was standing in the doorway, sun streaming through the hall windows backlighting her hair, lending her an almost supernatural glow.

'Hi,' he said, guarding against the leap he felt in his chest and the sudden urge to smile, lest it gave away his feelings about last night and this morning. 'What can I do for you?' Jonathan asked, instantly regretting how stuffy that made him sound.

'I...er, I've been looking at the accounts that you sent me and working through the numbers,' Rowan said. 'I was wondering if you still wanted to talk through it with me. I have a few ideas.'

'Oh, you're here to talk about work.' By the time he realised his face was showing how disappointed he was, it was too late to stop it.

Rowan grimaced, and he guessed that she hated how awkward this was too. 'I understand if you don't want to after last night...'

Had he really thought that she was here to give them another chance after what she had said in the kitchen? After she'd left that morning without a word? Maybe he should have gone to her and asked that they talk this through properly. They'd left things unsaid the first time that they had kissed, and he'd hurt her more than he'd known. He should know better than to avoid important conversations.

But he had gone into this knowing that he didn't have enough of himself to give to a partner to make a relationship work. Rowan deserved better than that. Deserved someone less distracted, less committed elsewhere. It would be too easy to let himself take what he wanted from her and ignore that he couldn't give her what she deserved in return. She had done them both a favour by giving what they had a clean ending. One that didn't hurt either of them.

An hour later, his back was aching from holding himself so straight and still while she talked through the financial options that she'd outlined on his laptop.

'The problem is,' Rowan summarised, reaching the end of her spreadsheet, 'that you can't go on as you are. You've been plugging holes, but you can't do that indefinitely. We need to find you a new source of income but it's not going to be easy to bring an investor on board a business that's failing—I'm sorry to be so blunt. But if we can show that we have viable plans to create the potential for a new revenue stream, we have a much better chance of securing the funds that you're going to need.'

'What are you thinking?' he asked, looking away from the figures on the laptop and meeting her eyes for the first time. She looked unsure of herself since they'd first started talking about the business, and he guessed that that meant he should brace himself for whatever was coming next.

Rowan clasped her hands together and rested her elbows on the desk. Her face had a determination that he hadn't seen before, but which he definitely liked. 'You know that Liv is excited about the research we found on the old fragrance line—well, so am I. That's exactly the sort of thing that could hook an investor. There are PR and publicity opportunities, and you really should consider using Liv's expertise. She's got the experience and the family name, and she's talented. She knows how to build excitement for a new brand. I think you know that this is a good idea. Your competitors are already doing this and making a lot of money from it.'

Jonathan nodded. He agreed with everything she had said. And if they were talking about anyone else's business, he would be telling them to start it yesterday. But this wasn't just business—he couldn't do this without getting Liv and Caleb involved, and he'd promised himself that he wouldn't do that. That he wouldn't burden them with the knowledge that they might lose the family business on top of everything else until it was inevitable. 'I know it's a good plan,' he told her. 'I trust you—I trust your judgement and your numbers—but I can't do this without telling Liv and Cal about the trouble that the business is in. I don't want to do that. They shouldn't have to worry about that. They've been through enough.'

Rowan gave him a sympathetic smile. He didn't deserve her pity. 'You shouldn't have to worry either,' she told him. 'But you do. And you shouldn't have to do this alone. Let them help you. Let them be a part of it. If this was someone else's business, you know what you'd be telling them.'

'Of course I would.' He'd had the same thought himself moments ago, and felt like a hypocrite arguing with Rowan about it now.

'I'd be telling them to take a risk, that they had no other choice. But *I'm* the one that would be looking their staff in the eye and telling them that they didn't have a job if all this goes wrong. I'd be the one telling my brother and sister that the family business went down on my watch, after more than a hundred years. We could lose everything.'

'Jonathan,' Rowan said gently, 'that's what's going to happen if you don't do anything.'

He shook his head, because surely there had to be some other way. 'But if I just—'

'What, find some more money from somewhere? It might help for a few months, and then you'll be right back here again.' She smiled, sympathetically, trying to soften the blow. He appreciated the gesture, but it didn't help, because he knew that she was right. She rested a hand on his shoulder, and he let himself draw comfort from it, even though he knew that he didn't deserve it. He couldn't keep taking from her like this when he had nothing to reciprocate with.

'So I should go down fighting?' he asked, his voice near to breaking.

'You should make sure you've considered

all the options before you make a decision one way or another,' she told him firmly.

'Did you do that with us? Consider all the options before you decided whether you wanted out?' He didn't know why he had said it. Why he had brought the conversation back to the topic that they'd been studiously ignoring for the past two hours. But the weight of all the things that they weren't saying—all the questions he had about why she had put an end to things that morning when they still had days and nights here that they could be enjoying together—was suddenly unbearable.

Rowan was evidently so shocked that she couldn't speak for a few moments.

'I… That's completely different,' she said. 'We were talking about work.'

He shook his head, not sure if he was apologising. 'I can't concentrate on work when I keep thinking about last night.' The words settled into the room around them, and he wasn't sure where they went from here. 'Look,' he said at last. 'Why don't we get out of here for a bit. I'm sick of these four walls, there's too much going on in my head to make sense of any of it and I can't talk to you properly when my brother or sister might walk in at any moment.'

She stared at him for a minute before nodding. 'Okay, I guess we've earned a break,' she said at last. 'Liv mentioned that there's a market in the town today. I wouldn't mind going for a look.'

'That sounds perfect.' Jonathan said, closing his laptop. 'I'll meet you in the hallway in five minutes.'

CHAPTER ELEVEN

THIS WAS SUCH a stupid idea. Her whole plan was to get over Jonathan. To kiss him, take what she needed from him. And then *move on with her life*. Because he was never going to be the one. Or, to be more specific, she was never going to be the one for him. He'd had every opportunity to fall in love with her and never once decided to take her up on it. Falling for him would be utterly reckless, and she knew it. She shouldn't have gone to bed with him last night.

But she couldn't make herself regret something so perfect. Something that had felt so right in the moment, and even now, knowing that it was a bad idea, *still* felt so right.

And instead of keeping her distance from him, like she had told herself this morning that she must, she had spent the morning poring over his company accounts to try and distract herself while Liv slept, two more hours talking through what she had found with him, and now she was picking up her backpack and slicking on some tinted lip balm so that they could go look at antiques and artisanal cheeses and local handicrafts.

They walked down the long, gravelled driveway towards the town, and Rowan had never been so aware of her own hands before. They seemed to swing at her side like great weighted balloons. This was stupid. If she wanted to hold his hand, she could just do it, but she knew deep down that she wouldn't. The only way that she could avoid getting her heart thoroughly trodden on was to try and forget that last night had ever happened. She had been perfectly clear with Jonathan that they were better off as just friends.

They were enveloped by an uncomfortable quiet as they walked, with just the wind-rustled leaves and tweeting birds interrupting the silence. She glanced across at Jonathan, only to find him looking back at her, and she blushed, fiercely, as she looked away again.

'Look,' Jonathan said at last as they

reached the first houses on the edge of the town. 'Tell me if you don't want to have this conversation. But last night being a one-off…is it really because of Liv? Or is it me? Is it something I've done?' he asked.

'What? No!' Rowan replied, genuinely surprised that he could think that this was anything that he had *done*. 'I just think it would be too complicated.'

It seemed easier to say than, *We both know that you're going to tap out of this first, and I don't think I can handle that again.* She was meant to be moving on, and she couldn't do that off the back of a heart broken for the second time.

'But you knew it was complicated yesterday,' he pointed out, not unreasonably. 'I'm not disagreeing with you or trying to change your mind. I'm just trying to understand what has changed since then.'

For the first time she felt ashamed of the fact that she had gone into this knowing that this was temporary for her, but without asking whether that was what Jonathan wanted too. He had made clear the first time they kissed that his interest in her had its limits—it was attraction, not something deeper. She hadn't even known that she had the power to hurt him. How could she know that, when up until now he had been the one doing the hurting.

It was just hurt pride that he was feeling, she told herself as they crossed a bridge over a small brook. Not a real wound. Not like he had hurt her. He would have forgotten about her in a matter of days. Not carry these memories round with him for years, until he had to take drastic action to get over it. So why did she feel guilty?

They'd reached the marketplace, the stone cross at its centre weathered with centuries of exposure to the elements. The steps at its base smoothed with use. The stalls were all covered with blue-and-white-striped awnings, customers crowding round each one. The smell of coffee from a tiny three-wheeled truck competed for her attention with the pop of a Prosecco bottle from a temporary bar in the centre of the square.

She turned to face Jonathan. 'I just think it's best if we forget about it.' He stared and stared at her, until she had to ask, 'What?'

'This isn't how I thought today was going to be,' he said at last, pinching the bridge of his nose.

'Oh? And how did you expect it to be?' She gathered her courage and decided to call his bluff. 'Were you planning on asking me to be your girlfriend?'

'We… I— No. Um… I thought that I'd made clear…' Jonathan spluttered, and Rowan gave him a sympathetic smile as she pushed him towards one of the stalls. *See?* she reassured herself. His ego might be bruised that he didn't get in there first, but he hadn't wanted this to be more than casual any more than she did.

Except, oh, it hurt to lie to herself. And just because she wouldn't let herself want any more than he was willing to give, that didn't mean that she wouldn't have wanted it if things had been different.

'Come on,' she said, pretending that it wasn't breaking her inside to have to be the one pushing him away. 'Let's not argue. There's tons here to explore. Where do you want to start?'

The stall behind them was loaded with mountains of olives in every variety she could think of, and more besides. The next was stacked with wheels of cheese, and the one after that with sausage rolls and Scotch eggs the size of her fist. By the time that they reached the antique stall at the end of the row, they were both toting little paper bags of goodies to take back to the house with them. And Rowan briefly allowed herself to entertain the thought that she could happily come back to this town, this market, every week for the rest of her life and be perfectly contented. And then tried to shake away the thought because that picture didn't make any sense without Jonathan in it, and she'd just told him that there was no way that was ever going to happen.

She did her best to shake off the melancholy and look properly at the antiques, because if you weren't going to do that when you were in the Cotswolds, when would you?

She gasped when the decorative glass bottles at the far end of the stall caught her eye.

'Oh, my goodness, are those—?'

'Perfume bottles?' Jonathan finished for her, following the line of her gaze.

He checked with the stallholder and then picked one up, handing it to her. She lifted the stopper and inhaled, hoping to catch a hint of the scent that it had once held. There were half a dozen of them in different styles.

Some cut glass, some coloured. One was decorated with a crown of tiny ceramic flowers.

'They're so beautiful,' she said with a smile. 'Do you think that this is a sign?'

Jonathan smiled at her, and she got the feeling he was indulging her a little. 'Maybe. We should take them home for Liv. Except for this one,' he said, taking the one that she was still holding, and passing it to the stallholder. 'This one's for you.' She smiled, wide and unabashed, and didn't care that her whole heart was on show. It was too tempting, being cherished by this man. He was too good at it. Making her feel like she mattered. She had to keep reminding herself that she would only get hurt if she let herself think like that. Eventually, he would push her away, and she knew that she couldn't survive that again.

They wandered among the other stalls, searching out their treasures, and when the sun reached the top of the roof of the pub at the other side of the market, Rowan sighed and suggested that they walk home.

'Tell me more about your race,' Jonathan

said, as they retraced their steps over the bridge and out of the centre of the town.

Rowan grinned, still more excited than nervous at the thought of her ultramarathon. The nerves would come later, when she was tossing and turning and struggling to sleep the night before. Counting down the hours before her alarm went off at five in the morning.

'It's an early start,' she warned him. 'And a long event. I'm not going to hold you to doing it if you've changed your mind. If you didn't really understand what you were volunteering for.'

'No, shush,' he said, a gentle hand at her elbow. 'I just want to know more about it. Why you love it. It sounds like torture to me: I didn't know that you were into that,' he added with a smile.

'Oh, I don't know, I've never really experimented,' she replied with a gleam in her eye that made him blush and then laugh. He nudged her with his shoulder, so she carried on talking.

'It's a hundred miles. Will probably take me about twenty-four hours. I've only done two before so it's sort of hard to judge. This will probably be the furthest I walk between now and the start line. I'll have to park myself in a chair for a couple of days. Conserve energy.'

'So you run through the night?' he asked.

'Yep. With a head torch and a map. And a compass. It can get a bit hairy, but I've always managed to find the finish line eventually.'

'And you run the whole way?'

She shrugged. 'It depends how I'm feeling. I might walk some of the bigger hills to save my legs. The important thing is to keep moving.'

'And what do you need me to do? Hand out energy bars and water bottles?'

Rowan nodded. 'And change batteries and make sure my phone is charged and find me dry socks. But…' She hesitated. 'Liv knows when to push me and when to listen and… she knows my limits. Knows what I can do.'

'I don't know you as well as she does,' Jonathan said, sounding worried for the first time.

'No,' Rowan agreed. 'But… We have a connection, right? I've not imagined that? I trust you to know what I will need.'

* * *

The words struck him right in the chest.

She trusted him to know what she needed from him. She might need him to make a call for her that she couldn't make for herself.

The thought of that should have filled him with dread. He should have been turning on the spot and walking away from a woman who was being completely open about the fact that she needed something from him. On paper, it looked like an obligation. A burden. But it didn't *feel* like that. It felt like something that he would willingly give— let her take—because they would be a team and he knew that she would do the same for him. Was this what she had been talking about? That he was the one who kept his relationships so one-sided. How he kept secrets from Liv to protect her, and in the process cut off his family, who should have been his greatest source of support over the last years.

They walked the rest of the way back to the house in silence as he thought over everything that Rowan had said, and the different paths for his future that she'd shined a light on.

'So you'll trust me with that but not with…' He let his voice trail off, but she knew exactly what he was talking about. He couldn't blame her for wanting to make her boundaries clear, but he couldn't shake the deep sadness that he felt at the idea that the night before might be a one-off. He wanted more of her. It had felt like the beginning of something, not the end.

But the beginning of something didn't have to mean the beginning of for ever, he reasoned. They were only here for a few more days. There was a natural end point built into this little rural idyll, so why didn't they make the most of it?

'Come on, out with it,' she said, looking across at him. 'What are you thinking?'

'Just that…we're leaving in a few days. So, anything that we start would naturally—'

'Come to an end,' she finished for him.

He nodded, glad that they were on the same page. Because suddenly the thought that everything he had shared with Rowan was in the past, that they were destined now to just grow further and further apart filled him with sadness. 'That's right,' he said. 'So we could…enjoy one another and then draw a line under it. If that's what we both wanted.'

He watched her carefully as a small smile crept from the corner of her mouth and he felt something in his chest ease, like he had staved off a heart attack.

'And that's what you want?' she said. 'Something temporary. Something we can draw a line under.'

No. He had to force himself not to say the word out loud. Because it wasn't what he wanted but it was all that he could risk. All that he could justify taking for himself. So he nodded.

'Yes. We enjoy ourselves while we're here, and then we go back to being friends.'

Rowan thought for a few minutes more. 'Define enjoy one another,' she said at last, with a defiant look in her eye.

He took a step towards her and trapped her chin between his thumb and forefinger, making sure she was looking him right in the eye. 'You look flushed,' he said, with a deadly serious tone of voice. 'Tell me what you were thinking just then.'

The corner of her mouth ticked up again. 'I wasn't thinking anything. If I'm flushed it's because it's so warm out,' she said, turning her face up to the sun before he brought her gaze back to his. 'I think I need to cool off a bit. Maybe I'll take a shower when we get back.'

His brain conjured the whole scene in the space between one heartbeat and the next. Water pounding on her shoulders, running over her breasts, sluicing down her belly. The click of the door and the slide of a shower screen. She'd keep her back turned, her eyes closed, as she waited for his arms around her waist pulling her back to him. He could feel the cold tile and hot water, her soft skin and the smooth slide of soapsuds.

He grabbed her hand and pulled, thankful that she was every inch as tall as him and could keep up with the near sprint as he dragged her up the drive.

'What are you doing?' she asked, laughing.

'Getting you home for that shower,' he replied, deadly serious. She gave him a self-satisfied grin, and he guessed that every thought he'd just had had shown on his face.

'I'll leave the door unlocked.'

CHAPTER TWELVE

THEY'D NEVER QUITE made it downstairs after the shower. God knew what Liv and Caleb thought was going on, Rowan considered as she got dressed the next morning. Actually, they probably knew exactly what was going on and that was why no one had asked. At least she could trust Liv not to ask questions she didn't want the answer to. Still, she supposed at some point she was going to have to talk to her best friend and figure out how their friendship worked now that she was sleeping with Liv's brother.

'Sleeping with' in the present tense, she acknowledged to herself, because any pretence she'd managed to maintain that she would be able to move on once she'd got Jonathan out of her system was long gone. But he'd pointed out that this week had a natural end point, and she was not going to argue with him. It was no different from a holiday romance, she reasoned to herself. She was going to enjoy him while they were here and then go back to her normal life, all sun-kissed and satisfied, warm with memories.

Lying in bed that morning, she and Jonathan had come up with a plan to tell his siblings about the problems with the business, and the possible solutions that were on the table. Jonathan was going to explain the financial difficulties the business was facing.

'So, what's this all about?' Liv said, cringing slightly as they all sat around the kitchen table. 'Is this all to tell me I'm getting a new sister?' she said, trying to force a laugh, and wincing as if she was preparing to hear something gruesome. Jonathan blushed and glanced at Rowan, who rolled her eyes.

'This is about Kinley,' Jonathan said, cutting straight to it. 'About your idea for the perfume. I want to explore the idea further and I want you to do it. I think we should give it a try, but there are some things that you need to know first.'

'About perfume?' Cal asked, looking dubious, as if he wished he could be back in his room rather than being dragged into family business.

'About the business. There are some things going on that I haven't told you about, and I should have done. The long and short of it is, there's no money to do this. There's no money for anything. If we want to launch a new product line, we're going to have to get finance from somewhere, and that's not going to be easy, considering the mess that the company is in.'

'How big a mess?' Liv asked, narrowing her eyes. Rowan just hoped that she could hold off her interrogation long enough for Jonathan to tell his side of the story.

'Very big,' Jonathan said with a sigh.

'And you've been trying to handle it all by yourself, which is why this is the first that we're hearing about it?' Liv guessed out loud, which showed she knew her brother better than he thought she did.

Jonathan nodded. 'I've been using my savings to keep us afloat but that's not an option any more.'

Understanding dawned in Liv's expression. 'So that's why you're selling the house,' she said. 'Because you need the cash.'

'I can't afford to keep it. And any profits from the sale I can use in the business. It's not what I want either, but there really isn't any other way.'

'Cal and I have savings,' Liv interjected. 'Why don't we use those, and keep the house?'

'And, you know, I have some bitcoin I invested in a while back,' Caleb added.

They all stared at him with wide eyes for a few moments before Jonathan brought the conversation back on track, shaking his head as he spoke. 'I can't let you sink your inheritances into the business.'

'Why not?' Liv asked, a little more heat in her voice. 'It's what you did with yours. Do you think that we don't care as much about the business as you do?'

'That money is for your futures,' Jonathan said firmly, and Rowan could see what direction this conversation was about to take and wasn't quite sure how to stop it, or if she should.

'The money was left to us to decide what we want to do with it,' Liv pointed out. 'I don't think that it's fair of you to tell me that I can't invest it in the family business. *Our* family business. The fragrance line was my idea. The least you can do is let me put my own money on the line.'

'What if you lose it all? I'm trying to protect you,' Jonathan told his sister gently, before Rowan laid a hand over his.

'Okay, let's take a breather,' Rowan said, looking at each of the siblings in turn. 'Jonathan, I don't think that you can tell your siblings what they can do with their money. If they want to invest it in the business, what better investors do you think you're going to find? Let's treat this like any other business decision. We'll write a business plan and see where we get to. Be as objective about this as we can. If you decide to look for investors, you should give Liv and Cal the chance if they want it,' she said.

And then she held her breath to see how her words landed. Whether Jonathan was going to give the people he loved the chance to support him for once, rather than pushing them away. Suddenly, the outcome of this felt much more pertinent to her future than she had ever wanted it to.

'Okay,' Jonathan said. 'Okay. Let's do the numbers and come up with a proper plan, and if you really want to take the risk, then I'm not going to stop you,' he said, sounding resigned. Rowan let out her breath. So he was going to try. It was a start.

Cal and Liv headed upstairs, muttering between themselves, leaving Jonathan and Rowan alone at the kitchen table. Rowan wanted to slide her hands into Jonathan's hair, turn his face up to hers and kiss away that despairing expression on his face. But she knew from the stiff line of his shoulders that that wasn't what he needed right now.

'I think that went well,' she suggested gently, wincing slightly when Jonathan snapped his gaze up to hers, making it clear that he didn't agree.

'I had no intention of them losing their own money in this,' he said, a sharp edge to his voice.

'You didn't think that they would want to help?' she asked. How could he not have seen that the suggestion might come up?

'I don't want them to lose their inheritance. I would never have suggested it if I'd known that this was how it was going to go.'

She sighed, because he might be showing some outward signs of growing out of this martyr complex, but right now he was showing who he was deep inside, and that person didn't seem to be open to change at all. 'At some point, Jonathan,' she told him sharply, 'you're going to have to accept that they are adults who are allowed to make their own decisions and take their own risks. Cal has a secret stash of bitcoin none of us knew about, for goodness' sake. Surely you should be happy to have willing investors, ones with as big an emotional stake in the company as you have? You couldn't ask for better partners. You don't have a monopoly on caring about the business or your family's legacy.'

'They're not my partners!' he said, standing and coming round to her side of the table. 'They're my...'

'Your what, Jonathan?' she prompted when he didn't finish his sentence. 'They're not your kids. They're not even your responsibility any more, at least no more than you are theirs. Why is it so impossible to accept that they're capable of making their own decisions? To let them help you, for once. Do you have such a God complex that you can't even let them stop your business from going under? You just expect all the people who love you to stand by and watch while you stress yourself into a heart attack because you're too proud to let anyone help you? We're here, Jonathan. I'm here. For you. We love you—I love you—and I want to help you and you won't let me. You're allowed to accept help. You're allowed to *ask* for it. You're allowed to let people love you and it doesn't make you a failure.'

That was it, everything she'd always wanted to say to him and more. She'd told him that she loved him. She hadn't even admitted that to herself until the words had been spilling from her mouth in a desperate attempt to get him to help himself.

'But I don't want that, Rowan,' Jonathan said, his voice broken. 'I can't let you love me, and I don't want to love you back, because you'd be just one more person I'd be letting down when this all falls apart.'

It wasn't how this was supposed to go. He was meant to protect his family. Protect his business. Protect Rowan by staying the hell away from her. And somehow in the space of a few days he'd managed to make everything so much worse on all three fronts. If he'd thought he had too much at stake before, it was nothing to where he found himself now, after his siblings and Rowan had conspired to convince him to take a risk that he almost certainly couldn't afford.

This was why he'd made the choices he had. The sacrifices he had. This was why he had torn himself away from Rowan the first time that he had kissed her and kicked himself until he remembered exactly why he wasn't allowed to have this.

And then he'd been stupid enough to forget. To convince himself while he was here, away from his real life, that this was something that he was allowed to have. He'd held Rowan close and refused to acknowledge the fact that it was never going to work out. That it could never last once they were away from this place.

He'd not even been able to keep it that long without messing up. Without dragging his family and his business into things as well until it was all so tangled that he didn't know how to fix one thing without something else unravelling.

And the worst of it all was that she was

in love with him. Or believed that she was. When he'd thought that he was the only one with their heart on the line, it had been bad enough. He didn't think that he'd be able to hurt Rowan so badly so soon. Which had been entirely his mistake, of course. He should never underestimate the harm that he can do to the people closest to him.

'I'm sorry, Rowan. I know that we said that we could enjoy this while it lasts, while we're here, but this has just proved everything I thought before we started. It was never going to work. I was never going to have space in my life to give you what you deserve, and it was foolish of me to even try.'

CHAPTER THIRTEEN

I DON'T WANT to love you back.

It shouldn't have felt like such a shock. She'd known, always known, that what she and Jonathan had was temporary. She'd managed to convince herself that *this* was who she was now. Someone Jonathan would never want to walk away from. And she'd been so distracted by that, so tempted by the thought that she might be someone he could want more than once, that she'd missed her opportunity to walk away before he could hurt her.

But she had told him that she loved him, and that hadn't even registered. Hadn't moved him one bit—and that utterly broke her.

The worst of it was, she couldn't even be angry with him. She'd known well enough that this would happen. She'd been relying on the fact that she was going into this thinking that she knew what she was doing. That she'd be able to keep her head and make rational decisions and… Oh. She had been completely deluded.

'You know what, it's fine,' she lied. 'We both knew that this was only going to last a few days so let's just forget it ever happened. Leave the whole thing behind us.'

'Don't pretend with me,' Jonathan said, sounding defeated. 'You just told me that you love me. Don't pretend that you're not hurt for my sake.'

'For God's sake, Jonathan. Stop trying to fix it! You don't want me. Fine. All I wanted was the chance to finally move on and forget that kiss. Well, I've got plenty of new mistakes to ruminate over now. Job done.'

He stared at her in a way that made her want to run, fast, but she fought the urge down, because she had been running and hiding from him for years, and she was tired of it now. They were going to have this conversation all the way to the bitter, inevitable end.

'That's what this was about for you? A chance to reject me and get your own back?'

he asked, his voice as hard as she had ever heard it. Which wasn't entirely fair. She was under no illusions over the mistakes that she had made. But she hadn't broken this…fling, relationship, whatever…up on her own. In fact, in the end, she hadn't done it at all. 'Then I really don't see how I am the villain here if this was never real for you.'

'I never said it wasn't real,' she objected. Certainly the pain that she felt in her chest right that moment felt as real as any other. 'For me, anyway. I never expected you to feel the same way.'

'Good, because I don't feel the same way. I hate the way I feel when we are together,' Jonathan said, as if he had deliberately chosen the most devastating comeback.

Rowan felt herself physically flinch. She took a step away, glancing over her shoulder at the doorway and wondering whether she should have just left the question unanswered. She should have walked away and left herself in her blissful, blissful ignorance.

'I wish that I could love you the way that you deserve to be loved. But I can't. There's not enough of me left to give, not without breaking me completely. I could never ask you to settle for so little.'

She huffed through her nose. Because, just once, couldn't he actually speak to her about what she wanted rather than just deciding for her? 'Ask me?' she said derisively. 'I don't remember you asking me anything. I remember you making an awful lot of assumptions about what I might or might not want.'

Jonathan stared at her for a moment, and she wondered which of her words he was struggling to process. In the end, he sat down, leaning back against the side of the table.

'What, and you're saying you did anything different when you walked out the morning after we slept together?'

She felt that one hit home, and when her cheeks burned this time, it was with shame. Had she been the one who had ruined this? Because she didn't trust him not to reject her again?

'I'm sorry, Rowan. You don't know how much I wish that things were different.'

'So do I,' she said sadly. 'I wish that you could understand that loving someone means letting them look after you too. I wish you knew how good we could have made this if you were willing to take a chance on it. On me.'

She felt her heart throb for him. For this kind, loving man who thought that he wasn't enough. Who gave so much of himself that he didn't realise that he could take as well. And then her heart broke, because she had put everything on the line here, to give herself a chance to move on. To think that one day she would let herself fall in love without her whole heart belonging to Jonathan, and she knew now that that would be impossible.

CHAPTER FOURTEEN

ROWAN WAS AVOIDING him and he should allow her that space, Jonathan told himself the next morning. He couldn't blame her, not after everything he had said the day before. He'd seen the look on her face when his words had landed, and he knew that he'd hurt her, even when he was trying to save her from himself. And he knew that he should leave her alone. He couldn't offer her what she wanted—what they both wanted—and it could only make things worse to keep prodding that wound. But he couldn't bear the thought that they were under the same roof and not speaking either.

He only had a few days with her, and even if they weren't spending them in bed, as he'd allowed himself to hope they might, that didn't mean that he didn't want to see her at all.

Perhaps it was selfish—probably, it was selfish—to go to her room just to see her, speak to her, given that he wasn't going to change his mind. But he found himself outside her door anyway, because it took more strength than he had to be where she wasn't.

Rowan supposed she should feel better now that she and Jonathan had been completely honest with each other at last. She looked over her drop bags for the ultramarathon, spread out on her bed. At least she knew now with absolute certainty that they didn't have a future. Jonathan didn't even *want* to fall in love with her, because he saw love as nothing more than a burden. If he fell for her, she'd just be someone else who he'd have to take care of, and hadn't ever considered that in loving him back she'd maybe give as much as she took.

Shouldn't she feel…better than this, now that she knew everything? She looked at the bags that she had spread over Liv's bed, individual bags full of snacks, spare clothes, blister plasters and batteries, one for each of the seven stops on her route. It would be the first race that she'd run without a crew—

she hadn't asked Jonathan whether he had changed his mind. He'd made it clear that he didn't want anyone else to look after, and she couldn't see him spending a full day in a field somewhere after the argument that they'd just had.

It was essential that she didn't miss anything. She lined up all the bags and dug around for the laminated checklist that she always put together before a race, but every time that she tried to concentrate on it, her mind wandered.

She hadn't known that it was possible to go from feeling so hopeful to so broken in the space of a day. God, she was going to need so much therapy when she got back to London, she groaned to herself.

After all, when left to her own devices, how had she done trying to fix her battered and broken self-esteem—she'd thrown herself into bed with a man who had already rejected her once, didn't want her now, made all their relationships endlessly more complicated, and then fallen in love with him. It was hard to imagine any therapist doing a worse job than that.

She heard footsteps in the corridor and

looked up to see Jonathan in the doorway. They'd been studiously avoiding each other since their argument earlier, and she still couldn't bring herself to meet his eyes. He seemed just as awkward, hesitating on the threshold for a few moments, and she wondered if he was going to bring up everything they had said to one another. 'Checking your kit?' he asked, and she felt disappointed all over again.

'Big day tomorrow,' she said with a false smile. She wouldn't let him see how much she was hurting. It was the only control she had left. He came over and took the checklist from her hands, gently prising it from her fingers and ignoring her quiet protests.

'You've already done this,' he said, looking down at the careful rows of check marks. 'It looks like you have everything you need,' he said.

She nodded. They could do this. She could talk about running. That was safer than talking about…anything else, really. 'I think so,' Rowan replied. 'I just need to make sure I know where everything is. If I can't find what I need tomorrow—'

'Then I'll find it for you,' he said, frowning. 'Isn't that what I'm there for? Unless you're saying that you don't want me to be, after—'

'I just assumed you wouldn't want to,' she interrupted, so taken aback that he was still planning on giving up his Saturday for her, after everything that had happened. She knew that her hurt was showing in her voice. Well, fine. She wasn't going to pretend not to be. She had offered Jonathan everything that she had to give, and he'd been too scared to take it. To even let himself want it. She was allowed to be hurt.

'Rowan, we're still friends,' he said, though the past day hadn't exactly felt very friendly. 'I want to be there for you.'

She had to force herself not to snort at that. 'But I'm not allowed to be there for you?' she asked. 'It's too unreasonable to think that this could be reciprocal, that we could be a team?' She looked him straight in the eye, refusing to back down. Because she'd decided that this mattered. Once upon a time, she'd hidden her feelings from him, and it had led to years of misunderstandings and embarrassment. She wasn't doing that this time.

And, well, maybe it was working. Because she heard what he was saying, that he didn't want her. But any idiot could say that he did. This wasn't about her and whether she was enough for him. This was about his issues and the way that he was letting them stand in between them and something that could be really good. Well, fine. But she wasn't going to pretend that she agreed with him.

'I can't go over this again,' he said. 'I'm coming with you tomorrow. Concentrate on your race. If you want to talk more when you're done, we can do it then.'

She stared him down, and realised she wasn't going to get more than that from him today. He looked utterly drained.

'Okay,' she agreed. And it irritated her that he was right. Tomorrow's race was as much a test of her mind as it was her body. She should be taking tonight to meditate. To rest. To see herself crossing that finish line over and over again so by the time that she set off tomorrow the race was half done.

Rowan nodded and did what he suggested, moving the bag from the bed to the floor and sitting in the divot it left in the duvet.

'Are you nervous?' he asked, coming to sit beside her.

She let herself have a sigh of relief. This felt...almost normal. 'I always am the day before. Can you please remind me why I'm doing this?'

He laughed, sudden and startling in the quiet house.

'Why you're running a hundred miles in a day? I wish I knew.'

'I know, I know.' She dropped her head into her hands. 'I don't have to do it,' she said, as she usually did around this point pre-race. 'I can just not go. No one would know. No one would care.'

'True,' Jonathan acknowledged, and she looked up. She'd been expecting him to just tell her to stop being silly, but he was actually thinking about what she'd said. 'What if you'd done that before the last one,' he asked at last. 'Do you regret running that race?'

Rowan groaned, because she knew that she wasn't going to be able to argue. 'No. You know that I don't. If I did I wouldn't have entered this one.'

'Well then.'

He nudged his arm against hers, before

realising what he had done and practically jumping away, putting space between them.

'You give quite the pep talk,' she added. 'Thank you.'

'You didn't need a pep talk. Just someone to listen, and I'll always do that.'

She forced herself to smile and wished that they were back in that place where it felt natural to do so, rather than strained. 'Thanks.'

When Jonathan left—she guessed he was sharing Cal's room—she set her alarm for five a.m., which would give her enough time to fret over the checklists in her drop bags one last time before she headed to the start line.

She was still staring at the ceiling when her alarm bleeped the next morning, and she swung her legs over the side of the bed, as if her phone had given her the permission she'd been waiting for to finally admit that sleep wasn't going to come. It could be worse. She'd had sleepless nights before races before. She pulled on her kit, trying to mentally prepare herself for the day to come. Reminding herself of the reasons she was doing this. To test herself. To find the limits of her body and her mind and push herself through them step after step after step. To prove to herself that whatever else it might be, her body was strong and capable and would not let her down, regardless of what she threw at it. She had followed her training schedule. She had nourished her body. She had prepared in every way that she could to get as far as she could today.

Her kit consisted of comfortable old tights that had run hundreds of miles with her. A lightweight jersey with smooth flat seams. Every detail considered, so that when she was eighty miles in and convinced that she couldn't make another step, she'd done everything in her power to keep herself going. She looked up at the sound of a soft knock.

'Ready?' Jonathan asked, his head appearing around the door.

'No,' she confessed.

'Yes, you are,' Jonathan replied. 'And you know you are. Now come on. Breakfast.'

When she got downstairs, she was surprised to find Liv and Caleb already in the kitchen.

'This is for you,' Liv said, holding out a

bar of home-made granola, and a handful of Ziploc bags with extra portions. She pulled her friend into a hug and squeezed her tight.

'You're going to be amazing,' Liv told her, pushing her away so she could get a good look at her. 'Enjoy it. Soak it in. You're ready for this.'

'I will. I will,' Rowan replied, feeling a little tearful. 'I'll be back here tomorrow with a shiny new medal.'

She gave Liv one last squeeze and then turned to go.

CHAPTER FIFTEEN

At the starting line

SOMETIME BEFORE THE starting gun fired he
lost her. He had watched her check her pack,
double knot her shoelaces and choose a play-
list, and although she was standing only a
few feet from him, she was already gone.
Out running the race already, and all he
could do was watch and wait.

Except, well, none of that was true, was it.
He'd actually lost her yesterday, when he'd
snapped and told her that he couldn't let
himself love her. He tried not to remember
the look on her face when he'd said that, like
he'd stuck his hand right inside her chest and
twisted her heart. But it was still dark out
and her face was all he could seem to see.

He watched as the light from her head
torch shrank smaller and smaller as she ran

from him, and he shivered. He had been so certain in the moment when he had told her that he couldn't love her. But now he was alone, and cold, and just as certain that he *did* love her, whether he wanted to let himself do it or not. She was a part of him. He could feel it as she moved further and further away from him. He glanced at his watch and tried to calculate how long it would be before he saw her again, before he could lay his hands on her shoulders and look in her eyes and know that she was okay.

Checkpoint One

Jonathan looked at his watch and then checked against the lists of expected times at the aid stations that Rowan had given him that morning. He wouldn't worry for another quarter of an hour, he told himself, even though it was fifteen minutes past the time that he'd been expecting Rowan to appear in the distance, running towards him. That was the deal that he had made with himself. When he finally saw her turn the corner, running down the track towards the aid station, he couldn't deny the flood of relief he felt. Or then the pride that immediately followed it.

She looked strong, her head high and her chest out. He was by her side before she pulled to a stop, offering her a drink and a granola bar. She took both, with a breathless word of thanks, and he walked with her towards the exit of the aid station, guessing that she wouldn't want to stop and lose her momentum at this early stage. He couldn't resist wrapping an arm around her shoulders, just to feel that she was really there, solid and present. To soak her up as much as possible before they reached the gates out of the station and he would be left waiting. Again. 'You're doing so great,' he told her as they approached the volunteer checking race numbers. 'Just keep doing what you're doing and I'll see you at the next one,' he told her as she ran through the exit of the station and back out onto the course.

It had all happened so fast that he was still a little dazed as he watched her run off down the road, wondering whether he'd even helped at all. She'd barely needed him—and he suspected that that wasn't what he wanted at all.

Checkpoint Two

Three hours later, he watched Rowan hobbling up the track towards the second checkpoint and felt a clutch of concern in his stomach. It had been thirty minutes since he'd fixed his eyes firmly on the track and refused to move until he had seen that she was okay.

And she wasn't. There was something wrong. She was only a quarter of the way through the race distance and yet she was limping and grimacing.

'What's wrong?' he asked, rushing up to her, wrapping an arm around her waist and helping her to a chair. 'Feet,' she said simply. 'Hurt.'

He unlaced her shoes, pulled off her socks and found the problem quickly. A seam had rubbed a blister on the side of her little toe, and Rowan hissed as he wrapped a plaster around it, replaced her socks with a seamless pair from her drop bag and retied her shoes.

'Have you eaten since the last stop?' he asked, and when she shook her head he tutted gently and held up a sandwich so she could have a couple of bites. He tucked a couple of snacks into the right pocket of her pack and pulled out her phone.

'Music or talking,' he asked.

When she didn't reply, he made an executive decision and cued up some Beyoncé, thinking that she needed the boost. And then there was nothing more he could do. He pushed her to one of the Portaloos, then to the exit of the station, and watched as she ran along the track, wishing he could be out there with her and resigning himself to another few hours of watching and waiting. This was exactly why he didn't want to love her. Because he had spent most of his adult life feeling like this about Liv and Caleb, about his business and employees. Every moment that they were out of his sight he was worrying about them. Whether he was going to be able to pay the wages bill. Whether he was doing a good enough job with Liv and Caleb.

He didn't want to have to feel that way about Rowan as well. But it wasn't like he didn't think about her already. Like he hadn't played that night they had kissed over and over in his head, wondering if there was anything that he could have done differently to avoid hurting her. Surely that would only get worse the more he let himself love her. He didn't have a choice with Liv and Cal. The responsibility that he felt for them had been dumped on him and he'd had no say in it. But with Rowan, it would be different. He would be *choosing* to feel like this, and he wasn't sure if he had the strength, regardless of how much he wanted it.

Checkpoint Three

Rowan had been in such bad shape the last time that he had seen her that Jonathan was almost dreading her arrival at the halfway marker, with hours to indulge his worst fears about her in physical and mental pain. So when she appeared at the end of the track looking strong and fresh and not in the least like a woman who had just run two marathons back to back, he didn't know quite what to make of her. He had the contents of her drop bag laid out on a towel, sweet and savoury snacks, water and energy drinks and energy gels, plasters and painkillers and a change of clothes. But all she did when she saw him was wrap her arms around his neck and hug him tight.

'Thanks for the soundtrack,' she said between deep, gasping breaths. 'It was just what I needed.'

'My pleasure,' he said honestly, taking a step away so that he could get a proper look at her and see if he could work out what she needed. He couldn't stop staring. She was radiating energy, her long, lean limbs shining with perspiration, her face flushed. He was so intensely proud of her, he wanted to look around and make sure that everyone knew how amazingly she was doing. How incredible she was.

'I need sugar and salt and then carbs. A lot,' Rowan declared, looking to him to find them for her. He handed over the food he had ready for her, and asked if she wanted to sit.

'Need to keep moving.'

He walked with her through another enclosure, adding bits and pieces to her pack, fitting her head torch and swapping out her phone and headphones for ones with fresh batteries, all while she got some calories and hydration inside her.

When they reached the exit of the aid station, he squeezed her shoulder and she turned to him with a huge grin on her face. 'We're smashing this,' she told him. 'Absolutely smashing it.' And he felt himself nearly burst with pride that she was letting him do this, to be a part of it, trusting him. She didn't *need* him. She could be out doing this on her own, and he would have missed out on being a small part of her huge achievement. It was an absolute privilege to be here for her, he realised. To feed her and make sure she was drinking and to remind her to put on dry socks. It wasn't a burden to take care of someone who needed you. It was an honour. And in that light, the last ten years of his life, the last few days of his life, looked entirely different. If he let himself love her—well, it was too late for that. If he let himself believe that they could be together, to try and make this work—is that what it would look like? That loving someone would bring joy, alongside its responsibilities. That the responsibilities that he carried would feel lighter if he had someone to bear them with him. That he and Rowan as a team could be as unstoppable every day as he felt today.

Checkpoint Four

The glare of the sun had started to fade when Rowan hobbled into the station just five minutes past the goal time on his laminated card, but Jonathan could tell that she had not seen him.

He half expected her to be disorientated and confused but when he approached her and asked her what she needed, what he saw in her face was focus and determination. 'Bathroom, then…food, something to drink,' she said, faltering slightly before making herself move again. While she was in the bathroom, he got her food and snacks and tried to anticipate anything else she might need.

She appeared back where he had laid out her gear and refilled her drinks bottles while she grabbed food and walked towards the exit. He watched her carefully and—remembering something he'd read on an ultrarunning blog—produced a can of Coke. She looked up as he opened the ring pull with a satisfying hiss of gas, and she stopped abruptly. With absolutely nothing to warn him of what she was about to do, she grabbed him, a hand on each side of his face, and kissed him hard on the mouth. 'This is the best idea anyone's ever had,' she told him, taking three long swigs of the drink. Then she handed the can back to him as they reached the exit of the aid station and headed back out on the course.

He stood and watched for a long time as she grew smaller and smaller, moving further and further away in the distance. She hadn't *needed* him. If he hadn't been here she could have grabbed what she needed without his help. But it brought him so much joy to be the one who could give it to her. That's what he wanted to do: bring her happiness. With cans of Coke and comfortable beds and by being someone who always, always listened when she told him what she wanted, and who worked it out for himself when she couldn't. He had never seen someone as focused and determined as she had been when she had headed back onto the route.

He'd given up hours ago trying to pretend that he didn't love her. He was only now starting to realise all the different ways that he did—he loved the way that she could fix her eye on a goal and push herself beyond what most people could endure to achieve it. She set superhuman goals and worked and trained and then simply endured until she had achieved them. And with that remarkable capacity for endurance, he wondered, could he possibly hope that whatever feelings she had for him might have endured his rejections and his stupidity? Might he still have a chance with her when all this was over?

He packed up their gear and headed to the final checkpoint with the embers of this hope burning warm in his chest, and he determined to feed them, just little by little. But first, he had a more important job to do, and that was to be and do whatever Rowan needed of him to get her through the rest of this night and the rest of this race. All he could do after that would be to tell her how he felt and hope for the best.

And then he had to watch her run off into the setting sun, and shivered, not sure what the night would bring.

Checkpoint Five

Jonathan was braced for another whirlwind stop at mile eighty, the last aid station before the end of the race, so as he watched the time on his phone tick further and further into the predicted window for the stop he grew more and more concerned.

What if something had happened to her out there? She had changed her emergency contact details to his mobile when Liv had hurt her ankle. But what if there was a mix-up? What if they couldn't reach him, or if Rowan was hurt by the side of a road somewhere and no one knew about it?

Then, just seconds before he had decided he would have to find a race organiser to ask, there she was, walking up the track, her shoulders rounded and her face wet with tears, reflecting the light from his head torch. He jogged to her and wrapped his arms around her on instinct, squeezing her tighter when she burst into fresh tears.

'What is it? What happened?' he asked, pushing her into a folding chair and forcing a hot cup of tea into her hands.

'I can't do it,' she said, sniffing back tears and wiping her face with the back of her hands. 'I can't do it.'

'Okay, okay,' Jonathan said, holding the

hand that wasn't wrapped around her mug and pressing a kiss to the back of it.

He tried to think fast, wishing they had covered what to do in this situation— he didn't want to second-guess what she wanted. But he didn't want to let her down if all she needed was someone to tell her to get back out there. She had been so focused at the last checkpoint that he had never anticipated this.

'Tell me why you started,' he said, asking the first question that came to mind. 'Tell me why you run.'

'To see if I can,' she replied in a small voice, and he nodded. 'What a stupid bloody reason.'

'It's not stupid. And you can. You've run eighty miles already. That's more than most people can even imagine. A *regular* marathon is more than most people can imagine running. So why a hundred?'

She sat up a little straighter as she considered the question.

'Because I wanted to prove to myself my body wouldn't let me down. Even if I threw the hardest races in the world at it.'

He couldn't help but smile at that.

'And has it let you down?' he asked.

He couldn't tell her what to do—only she could decide that. All he could do was ask questions so he could try and understand her. Try and understand how to support her. She shook her head.

'Everything hurts,' she sniffed, and her voice was so small that something inside him broke. He pulled her to him for another hug.

'Does it always hurt after eighty miles?' he asked, tipping her face up and brushing the hair back from her face, clipping it back with the grips that it had escaped.

'Of course it does. But...'

'But?' he asked.

Rowan grimaced, like she didn't want to hear her own answer. 'But sometimes I run through it. Sometimes it doesn't matter that it hurts—I just do it anyway and then it's over.'

He thought about that for a moment. 'Do you want to run through it tonight?' he asked.

Rowan shook her head. 'I don't know. I don't know if I can.'

'You don't have to know,' he told her gently.

'You don't have to think too far ahead. Can you do another step, another mile?'

She nodded.

'Do you want to?'

She hesitated, and for a moment he thought that that was it, they were done. But then she got a look in her eye that was unmistakeably Rowan—battle ready—and nodded again and finished her tea.

'You can do this,' he told her earnestly. 'I've never seen something as incredible as you have been today. You endure like no one I've ever met before. You're strong and you're capable and you're amazing. You've been preparing for this for months and months and all you have to do is trust in yourself. Trust your body to do what you know it can do. I believe you can do it.'

She nodded again, eyes fixed now. Barely seeing him. He couldn't have cared less. Not a single moment of this was about him, no matter how his feelings for her had changed through the day, and the night. This was about Rowan. About helping her to be everything that she could be.

'I can. I can do it. I'm going to do it. I have to do it.'

She stood abruptly, knocking over the flask of tea and making him laugh. 'Steady on, sweetheart. Take a breath.'

He stuffed spare batteries, gels and blister plasters in her backpack and unscrewed the lids on her drinks bottles so the volunteers could fill them without costing her any more time. 'Your feet okay?' he asked, and she nodded, her eyes and her mind, he guessed, already back on the route. He pushed her towards the bathroom, forced a few spoonfuls of food into her and then pushed her back out into the dark night hoping that he had done the right thing.

The finish line

By the time the sun had started to rise, he'd managed a few hours' sleep in twenty-minute bursts, folded uncomfortably into a plastic chair, close to one of the small fires they'd lit for a little light and warmth. The festival atmosphere had quieted, and the time between runners arriving in the camp had stretched out, until each one was an event in itself, and they all pitched in to try and keep them running. He watched the sun come over the horizon, unable to think of anything but Rowan.

His alarm went off to alert him that they were approaching the finishing window. Given the state that Rowan had been in at the last checkpoint, he'd been expecting a call to say she was at the side of the road somewhere and would he come pick her up. But he had to assume that no news was good news and started to pull together what she might need when she was done.

And then he joined the small crowd still waiting and watching the approach to the finish line. Twenty-four hours ago, he had sent Rowan out into the unknown, with no clue that he would have fallen heart over gut in love with her by the time she was back.

But now wasn't the time to be thinking about his feelings for her. The only thing that mattered right now was getting her back safe and well. He checked his watch against the timecard. Still plenty of time. He abandoned his post just for a couple of minutes to get a fresh flask of tea from the van. His last twenty-four hours had nothing on Rowan's, but they hadn't exactly been the most restful or comfortable either, and both a little warmth and a lot of caffeine were needed right now.

And just as he was about to drop into his seat to resume his vigil, there she was, turning the corner of the lane. Her feet were barely leaving the ground as she took short, shuffling steps towards him, but she was still moving, still running, and he was still falling harder and harder for her by the second, seconds which seemed to crawl by as he waited by the finish line, cheering and whooping and clapping and desperate to have her back whole and safe.

She staggered straight into him across the finish line and he clutched her so tight that he lost his balance, and her legs gave out at the same time he was trying to find his centre of gravity. Without him knowing exactly how it happened they were in a heap on the floor with Rowan sprawled on top of him.

While he was still clutching for something to say, Rowan burst into both tears and laughter simultaneously, leaving him flailing for how to react.

Eventually, when helpful volunteers appeared in his peripheral vision to help them up from the ground, he managed to wave them off, roll her to the side of him, prop himself up on his elbow and look her over and make sure that she was all in one piece and that the tears were of relief and of nothing more serious. He brushed her hair back from her face, and she managed a weak smile, though she looked dazed and not entirely present.

'You did it,' he said, bursting with pride.

Rowan laughed aloud. 'I did it. At least I think I did. If I'm not hallucinating. Is this real?'

'Very real,' he said, wiping away more tears that she seemed to be unaware of. 'You really, really did it.'

And with that, she grabbed him by the hair and kissed him hard. He couldn't help but laugh against her lips as a couple of wolf whistles sounded behind him. He eased her hands from behind his head and knelt up on the ground, pulling Rowan upright.

'You need to drink something, sweetheart,' he told her. 'And then eat something, and then sleep for a week,' he told her firmly.

He looped her arm around his shoulders and walked her to his camping chair, where he could take care of her properly. After twenty-four hours of not knowing where she was, how she was, he just wanted to soak in the fact that he had her in his sight for the next twenty minutes, or twenty days, or however long she'd let him be there. Because there was no way that he was walking away from her. He loved her—nothing had ever been more obvious. And nothing could be clearer to him than that being allowed to love her and care for her and take care of her was a privilege—one that he could never tire of. He had seen her strength over the course of the past twenty-four hours, but even if she didn't have apparently superhuman strength and endurance, he knew that they were stronger together. That he wanted to face his future with Rowan in his life, and for him to be in hers.

Now he just had to try and convince her that he knew what an idiot he had been, that he was sorry and beg her to give him another chance.

But that could wait. Right now all he wanted to do was take care of her, so he fed her and hydrated her and helped her into warm clothes and was content to just watch her rest for a while until she started nodding and the cup of tea in her hand tipped precariously towards her lap. 'That's it,' he said with finality. 'I'm taking you home: you need to sleep.'

In her exhausted state she let him half carry her to the car, and she made soft, appreciative noises as he opened the door and helped her into the seat. She was snoring before they even reached the road.

CHAPTER SIXTEEN

ROWAN WOKE TO the sound of a creaking floorboard.

'Hello?' she called out, not quite up to opening her eyes yet. She wasn't on the back-breaker, that much was clear. But this didn't smell quite like Liv's room either. Which meant... She opened her eyes, and found Jonathan watching her from the doorway of his own bedroom.

'I'm sorry, I didn't mean to wake you,' he said.

She shook her head, because honestly she wasn't sure that he had. Truth be told, she wasn't even sure that she was awake or not. She had a horrible feeling that her memories of kissing Jonathan hard, even after they had talked endlessly of all the reasons he didn't want to be with her, weren't a dream. Something inside her chest threatened to curl up and die, but she forced herself not to show it on her face. Hopefully Jonathan could write it off as some sort of exhaustion-induced delirium.

'You've been out for a while,' he said now, leaning against the door frame. 'I just wanted to check you were okay.'

'I'm fine,' she said, and then tried to sit. At which point every single muscle in her body protested, and she decided that she was probably okay lying down a little longer. 'Maybe not completely fine,' she conceded. 'I'm in your bed again,' she said, realising that she had no memory of how she got there.

Jonathan nodded. 'You fell asleep in the car. I did try and wake you but you were insistent that you weren't moving and I couldn't let you stay out there after everything that you've been through. So. Here you are.'

'You carried me?' Rowan asked. She risked the pain of throwing her arm up to cover her face, because she couldn't bear the thought of him being that close to her while she looked, and smelled, like this. 'I'm disgusting.'

'No, you're lovely. I'm in love with you.'

At that she sat bolt upright, aching muscles be damned, and then groaned, loudly, as every single one of her abdominal muscles punished her for it.

Jonathan's hand was over his mouth, as if he couldn't quite believe what he'd just said. 'I— I'm so sorry,' he stuttered, crossing the room and sitting on the edge of the bed. 'I didn't mean to say that.'

'You didn't mean it?' she asked, terrified that he was about to take the words back, because she had been waiting to hear them for so, so long, and she wasn't sure she had the energy for mental gymnastics today.

'No! I mean, yes. I just mean…this isn't about me,' Jonathan said. 'This is your day. It shouldn't be about my feelings. I was going to say that I'd run you a bath.'

She laughed, a little weakly. 'Honestly, Jonathan. As delicious as a bath sounds, I think I'd rather know whether you're in love with me. And, if you are, what you're planning on doing about it.'

He hesitated, and then reached for her hand. She didn't even know whether she wanted to let herself hope. She was too tired, too drained. But apparently no one had told her heart, which had kicked back into race pace, and was waiting eagerly to hear where this was going. 'I... I am. I'm in love with you. I'm sorry.'

And as much as she wanted to let her heart sing and clouds to part, and angels descend, she couldn't quite get there. 'Why do you keep apologising?' she asked, and she could hear the tension in her own voice. 'Why do you have to be sorry that you love me? Why does it have to be so hard, Jonathan?' Maybe she would have guarded her words better if she hadn't been utterly wracked with exhaustion. Or maybe she should have all her conversations when she was too tired to filter. Too tired to lie.

'Because I've already told you how impossible I am,' Jonathan said, with a touch more regret in his voice than she wanted to hear. 'How difficult I'm going to make this.'

She stopped him with a hand on his arm and opened her eyes wider. 'This?' she asked, because she had to know what he was talking about. What he was offering, if he was offering anything beyond the knowledge that he loved her.

'This. Us. If you'll have me,' he said, and that sounded so much like everything that she had ever wanted that she still couldn't let herself believe it. 'I love you, Rowan. I have for such a long time. And in the past few days I have seen over and over again how strong you are and how capable, and I can't believe I ever tried to take a decision out of your hands. So if you'll have me, I'll try. Because I think that all I want is to be there for you, for your whole life, and to let you be there for me too. If you want to, that is.'

She stared at him, still not quite sure that she was really awake. That she wasn't still out there at mile ninety-two, hallucinating. Because this was everything that she had ever wanted. Everything she was afraid that she would never have—it had seemed so close a few days ago, and then further away than ever. And she still couldn't quite trust that it wouldn't be snatched away the minute that she admitted how much she wanted it to be true.

'And you realised all this…when I look like this?' she asked at last. Which wasn't exactly the most important part of this whole scenario, but it made it all so much less believable that she couldn't not address it directly. She looked down at herself, not quite sure what she was going to see. She was still in the soft sweats that he'd coaxed onto her when she'd finished the race, her medal still around her neck.

'You wouldn't let me take it off,' he said with a soft chuckle.

She stroked it. If the medal was real, then she really had finished the race. Which meant that she was really here, and… 'You love me?' she asked, just wanting to be really very doubly sure that she hadn't got that part wrong. 'And you're just going to…let yourself love me?'

'I love you,' he said, and his voice was surer now. 'And I'm not saying that I'm not terrified, but I'm much more scared of a life without you in it.'

She groaned, and even in her state she was sure that that wasn't the right reaction. 'I love you too, Jonathan, you know that I do,' she said from behind the hands she appeared to be covering her face with.

Until Jonathan pulled them gently away and met her eyes.

'Then why does that sound like a no?' he asked.

'It's not a no. It's just… Let's think about this, logically, I mean. Yesterday…the day before… I've lost track. But you were very clear that a relationship wasn't what you wanted. And you've just been more than twenty-four hours without sleep and accidentally told me that you loved me instead of telling me that you were running me a bath. It's just hard for me to trust that this is really what you want. What if I *do* say yes and then you get a good night's sleep and realise you've made a huge mistake?'

He nodded, and she could tell that he understood why she was holding back. 'I know what it looks like, sounds like. And I know that I've messed you around, Rowan. I absolutely do not deserve another chance and I completely understand if you don't want to give me one. But it's true, Rowan. Every word of it. I want this. I want you, more than anything I've ever wanted in my whole life. And I'm not pretending that I'm not utterly terrified at the thought of how we're going to make this work. I just know that I want to make it work with you, rather than without you.'

'I *want* to believe you,' Rowan said. More than she'd wanted just about anything else.

'You were right,' Jonathan went on. And okay, maybe she'd just keep letting him talk while she rested her eyes. 'Everything you said the other day when I was being a complete idiot and a coward. I don't give Liv and Cal enough credit. I've never seen my position as something that I'm blessed with, rather than something that I'm encumbered with, and I'm a complete idiot for insisting on doing things on my own for so long.

'It shouldn't have had to take watching you put yourself through what you did yesterday to make me realise it. But I was so proud of you. So grateful that you let me be even a small part of it. I like being a team with you, Rowan. I want to spend the rest of my life being a team with you.'

She watched him, the man she loved, as the torrent of words flowed from him. It all came down to one thing, really, and that was whether she could trust him. He had given her every reason before today not to. He had hidden his feelings and fudged his words and avoided her. But if she wanted proof that things were going to be different now, here it was, right in front of her. Telling her exactly how he felt, and how hard he was going to try. She would be a fool if she walked away now.

'I should have realised a long time ago that my life is so much richer and kinder and stronger with you in it and I can only hope that you can let me prove to you how much I love you and how much I want to be there for you. Whatever we're doing. Whether it's business or running or family, I want to do it all together, Rowan. I can't imagine doing any of it without you. Except no, I can. Because that's what I've been doing all these years and it's been miserable. And I've been happier this week with you than I've ever been before in my life and I can't believe that I was stupid enough to think that I could just walk away from that.'

Jonathan carried on talking, because he had no idea she'd already decided there was no way that she was letting him go. 'I'm sorry,' he added, when Rowan eventually put her hands to his face and kissed him, if only to make the words stop coming.

'You can stop,' she told him gently. 'I believe you. I believe that you love me, and that you want to make this happen.'

He nodded, his turn to be open-mouthed and speechless now.

'I'm… This is a lot to take in,' Rowan said, though she twisted away when his kisses trailed down to her neck. 'And I feel disgusting. Just…let me think? Give me a little time?'

'Of course,' Jonathan said into her collarbone, before looking up at her. 'Would it help if I actually ran you that bath?' he asked, and Rowan all but whimpered with anticipated pleasure.

'Run me a bath and I might marry you,' she said, her voice a little dazed. She winced—she had meant it as a joke, but maybe it was too soon for those sorts of throwaway comments. But Jonathan didn't even flinch and Rowan widened her eyes. Was that…on the cards? He just smiled and asked her something about bubbles in her bath as he crossed to the bathroom door and she desperately tried to struggle out of bed, her brain still trying to process everything that he had just told her.

She hadn't even thought beyond the bath that she could hear running in the next room, never mind where she and Jonathan might be a week or a month from now. But with that last smile of his, she realised that this actually had a future. They could start thinking about what they wanted their life together to look like and then just…make that happen.

CHAPTER SEVENTEEN

ROWAN LET OUT a long, low sigh as she leaned back in the tub, letting the water take the weight of her limbs and finally feeling some of the ache draw out of them.

'I'm in here,' Rowan called when she heard Jonathan walk back into his bedroom. She glanced down to check that the thick, foamy bubbles were protecting her modesty—which was maybe a bit horse and stable door et cetera—and then saw Jonathan appear and then hesitate in the doorway.

'It's fine,' she told him. 'I'm decent, you can come in.'

His eyes widened, so perhaps her idea of decent and his weren't quite meeting in the middle. But, honestly, she could look at that expression on his face all day—as long as she was the one putting it there.

'I made you a cup of tea,' he said. 'I was going to leave it in the other room.'

'It's okay. Stay, sit if you like,' she said.

So he did, on the floor, leaning against a vanity cabinet, his head level with hers, the rim of the tub hiding her body from his eyes, so that he finally looked like he might be able to have a conversation without being fatally distracted.

'I've been thinking about what you said,' she told him. Because how was she meant to think about anything other than him declaring his love for her. Especially when she was in the most delicious bath of her life—that he had run for her—just minutes after declaring his love. She let out an involuntary sigh of pleasure. If things didn't work out, would she be able to keep him just for this? But no, that would never be enough for her. She wanted him, all of him, and she wanted to keep him for ever.

'I knew I was in love with you before the race,' she told him. 'And even when you said that you didn't want to try, I knew that it wasn't about me.'

'Of course it wasn't—'

'No, wait, will you let me say this please?'

Rowan said. They'd spent years not talking about the way that they felt about one another, and it had hurt them both. She wasn't going to go into this with anything left unsaid. 'I've felt that way about you for a long time. At least since we kissed that first time, and probably before that. And I never in my wildest, most fanciful dreams thought that you would ever feel the same way about me.'

He opened his mouth to protest, but she leaned forward, resting her forearms and her chin on the edge of the bath, anything to be closer to him. 'I just looked at myself, and I heard everything that my bullies had ever told me, and I looked at *you* and I thought— of course he's not going to want me back. When you pushed me away that first time, it proved every bad thought I'd ever had about myself.

'And then any time I tried to be with someone else, they…they weren't you. So they were never what I wanted.

'Being here with you this week, I saw something in you that I'd never let myself see before. I saw how deeply you were hurting, and that your issues weren't with me at all—it was all about you trusting yourself to be able to do this. So I need to tell you this, and I need you to believe me if we're going to work: I know you, Jonathan Kinley. I know that you are kind, and thoughtful, and you care about me, and you know *me*. Yesterday wouldn't have worked if you didn't. And so I'm going to believe you when you say you love me. I'm going to trust you when you say that you mean it. And I'm going to do everything I can, for as long as you'll let me, to make sure you know I feel the same way. And if you start doubting yourself, and thinking you need to carry the whole world on your shoulders, and thinking that you're not good for me, or that *we're* not good for you, then you have to promise to talk to me about it.'

Jonathan rose to his knees in front of her, and she suddenly felt incredibly naked in a way that had absolutely nothing to do with the fact that she was in the bath.

'I promise. I meant every word I said,' he said, slightly breathless. 'I love you. I'm going to tell you again and again and again. Until you're sick of hearing it. And while I'm at it I'm going to tell you that you're brilliant and beautiful and so strong. And I'm thinking that I'll tell you that for ever, if that's okay.' He leaned forward, through the steam spiralling up from her bath, smoothed damp tendrils of hair from her cheeks and brushed the softest of kisses to her lips.

'I'm not sure for ever will be long enough,' she whispered between kisses, her hands curling into the front of his T-shirt. And then she pulled him into the tub, clothes and all, and squealed as a wave of water cascaded over the side.

He blinked down at her, his face a picture of surprise. His lips a soft O, his eyes wide and startled.

'Will you marry me?' he asked, still with that dazed expression.

Rowan managed to get her arms round his waist, her hands to the hem of his T-shirt, the sopping wet fabric somehow over his head and onto the floor.

'I think I asked first,' she reminded him as she pushed her hands into his hair and pulled him down for a kiss.

When their skin was wrinkled and the hot water tank empty, they admitted defeat and reluctantly left the bath. And then when they had towelled themselves, and each other and the bathroom floor, dry, they found themselves back on Jonathan's bed, on crisp clean sheets, curled around one another in the warm sunlight that found its way in through the diamond-patterned windows.

'So, we should probably tell Liv about this,' Jonathan said.

'Oh.' Rowan looked up at him from where she had tucked herself under his arm. 'You're right. Just as soon as I'm ready to leave this bed I'll talk to her.'

'I don't even want to think about what her reaction to me asking you to marry me is going to be.'

'Uh… I'll be telling her that *I* asked *you*,' Rowan corrected him, because she didn't want him thinking that this had happened all on his terms. 'And you still haven't answered, by the way. I proposed to you and you left me hanging.'

Jonathan turned on his side and propped himself on his elbow, his hand stroking a long line up her side. She blushed under his scrutiny but didn't look away. 'No, I didn't,' he said. 'I proposed back.'

Rowan rolled her eyes. 'That is absolutely not the same thing as accepting.'

He stared down at her and she grinned.

'Ask me again,' he said, brushing his knuckles across her cheek, letting his hand drop to her shoulder, nudging at the strap of her tank top. She bit her lip, not quite able to believe that she was doing this. That it was real.

'Jonathan, will you marry me?' she asked, her voice no more than a whisper. She reached for him, her arms around his waist, as she waited for his answer.

'Yes, I'll marry you,' he whispered in her ear, before kissing her on the sensitive skin just behind. 'I'd do it over and over and over again if I could.'

Rowan laughed into his neck. 'I think just the once will do it.'

'Okay, then,' he said, pressing her onto her back, holding her to the mattress with his body and kissing her hard. 'This. I want to do this every day of my life. Would that be okay?'

'I think I can probably live with that,' Rowan conceded with a sigh.

'Good.'

CHAPTER EIGHTEEN

THEY WALKED OUT to the maze that afternoon in a weak effort to make her legs move again, strolling slowly in the last warmth of the day, their fingers intertwined and swinging between them.

'Tell me you were going to kiss me in there or I'll always wonder,' Rowan demanded as she pulled him towards the entrance, untangling their fingers so that she could wrap her arm around his waist and lean into him.

Jonathan sighed and squeezed her side. 'Of course I was going to kiss you,' he said, leaning in and doing it now, slowly, until she was ready to drag him somewhere secluded. 'I feel like I've been about to kiss you since you appeared in my hallway,' he said. 'I've thought about you so often that for a minute I thought that I'd imagined you.'

'Mmm, I like hearing you confess things like that,' she said. 'Though it makes me sad that we didn't figure all this out sooner.'

Jonathan shrugged. 'We had to wait until we were ready,' he said, turning her face to him for another kiss. 'And we can make up for lost time now. I hope you don't want a long engagement.'

She broke away with a smile and pulled him into the maze. 'Maybe we should get married in here,' she said, walking backwards and pulling him by both hands. 'I think I was right when I said it was magical. And it feels like our place now.'

Jonathan smiled ruefully. 'Well, I don't know how much longer we're going to be able to. The estate agents are coming next week to take photos for the listings.'

'That's still happening?' she asked gently.

His eyebrows pulled together, and she rubbed away the creases between them with her thumb. 'I really don't think I have a choice.'

'Caleb can't buy it off you with his mystery bitcoins?'

Jonathan laughed. 'I'm really going to

have to ask him some questions about that, aren't I?'

'If you don't, I will. You never told me your brother has hidden depths. And he's cute too.'

Jonathan shoved her gently. 'Don't joke. It's bad enough that Liv gets first dibs on you.'

'Yeah, well, it's not my fault it took you so long to realise you were in love with me.'

He groaned, pulling her in tight to him and tweaking her ponytail. 'Don't remind me how much time I've wasted,' he said into her hair.

Rowan leaned back and kissed him on the lips. 'I'll forgive you if you promise there will be no nonsense about taking money from your siblings—because if you put the house on the open market they could just buy it off you with a lot more hassle if you really wanted to be mean about it.'

He nodded, and looked her in the eyes. He wasn't messing around, and she had never been so glad to see him so serious. 'I'll hear them out. I promise. The three of us—the four of us—will make a decision together. I've got no plans of being more of an idiot with my family, or with you, than I already have been. And if it helps, I fully expect you to take Liv's side if I'm causing problems.'

She smiled, because she hadn't quite got her head around how this was going to work yet, her best friend and her…fiancé, competing for her affection. 'Oh, that was never in question,' she told him. She could foresee a long night with Liv and several bottles of wine in her near future, just as soon as she could stand up from a sofa without groaning, and could go more than ten minutes without feeling she needed a full plate of carbs and two pints of water.

Jonathan led her through the maze easily this time, and they were soon in the sunlit clearing in the centre, the rose-covered love seat exactly as she remembered it.

'You're right. This place is ours now,' he said, wrapping his arms about her waist and resting his chin on her shoulder. 'I don't think I can let it go.'

'Because we didn't kiss here?' she asked, turning her head to give him a kiss and a wry smile.

'Well, we can put that right now,' he said,

dragging her over to the love seat. 'Hand me your phone?'

Rowan hesitated. 'What, why? Are you planning on documenting this?'

'No,' he said, taking it from her and turning it off before wrapping his arms around her again. 'Because I'm not taking any chances of being disturbed this time. I want you all to myself.' He pulled her into his lap on the swing and she let out a long, contented sigh, relaxing her body into his chest. She let her eyes drift closed and turned slowly in his arms, tipping her face up to his with a certainty and confidence she hadn't believed that she was ever going to find. And his lips met hers with an honesty that she was sure he'd never allowed himself before.

It was a kiss that told her everything about how he felt about her. How hard they'd fought to get here, to find one another. To overcome all the fears that had told them to walk away. It was a kiss that promised a lifetime together, and she was going to spend every day of that lifetime grateful for this man.

* * * * *